Q# 110116

THE TIGER'S APPRENTICE

BOOK THREE
TIGER MAGIC

The Earth Dragon Awakes
Sweetwater
When the Circus Came to Town
The Dragon Prince
Dream Soul
The Lost Garden
The Magic Paintbrush
The Rainbow People

DRAGON OF THE LOST SEA FANTASIES
Dragon of the Lost Sea
Dragon Steel
Dragon Cauldron
Dragon War

CHINATOWN MYSTERIES
The Case of the Goblin Pearls
The Case of the Firecrackers

EDITED BY LAURENCE YEP
American Dragons
Twenty-Five Asian American Voices

THE TIGER'S APPRENTICE

BOOK THREE

TIGER MAGIC

LAURENCE YEP

HarperCollinsPublishers

Tiger Magic
Copyright © 2006 by Laurence Yep
All rights reserved. Printed in the United States of America.
No part of this book may be used or reproduced in any manner whatsoever
without written permission except in the case of brief quotations embodied
in critical articles and reviews. For information address
HarperCollins Children's Books, a division of HarperCollins Publishers,
1350 Avenue of the Americas, New York, NY 10019.
www.harpercollinschildrens.com

Library of Congress Cataloging-in-Publication Data
Yep, Laurence.
    Tiger magic / Laurence Yep.— 1st ed.
        p.   cm. — (The tiger's apprentice ; bk. 3)
    Sequel to: Tiger's blood.
    Summary: A Chinese American boy and his band of friends must protect
the magical phoenix and fight a war to prevent the evil Vatten from taking
over the world.
    ISBN-10: 0-06-001019-3 (trade bdg.) — ISBN-13: 978-0-06-001019-5
(trade bdg.)
    ISBN-10: 0-06-001020-7 (lib. bdg.) — ISBN-13: 978-0-06-001020-1 (lib.
bdg.)
    [1. Magic—Fiction. 2. Phoenix (Mythical bird)—Fiction. 3. Chinese
Americans—Fiction. 4. San Francisco (Calif.)—Fiction.] I. Title. II. Series:
Yep, Laurence. Tiger's apprentice ; bk. 3.
PZ7.Y44Thu 2006   2005019074
[Fic]—dc22   CIP
                                                                                    AC

Typography by Karin Paprocki
1 2 3 4 5 6 7 8 9 10
❖
First Edition

To Bill Morris,
who was a wizard in his own right

PREFACE

This series really began more than thirty years ago when I began exploring my Chinese roots. I researched the Chinese American history that became *Dragonwings*, *Dragon's Gate*, and the other novels of the Golden Mountain Chronicles; and I was also reading Chinese mythology. I wanted to know not only the stories about the people in Chinatown but also about the statues that I'd seen on temple altars and on my grandmother's bureau.

I studied the *Shan Hai Ching* (ca. third century B.C.), a compendium of wonders that drew from earlier material like the stories about the Monkey King. I was surprised when I realized that those statues represented only the surface layer of a mythology that was more than four thousand years old.

CHAPTER ONE

The Pi-pi
She looks most like a fox with wings and honks like a wild goose.
When people see her, they know a terrible drought is coming.
—Shan Hai Ching

The Phoenix
The King of all birds has feathers as red as cinnabar and appears
only in times of peace and justice. It is said to have the power to
make evil creatures good.
—Tradition

The Chinatown antique store seemed as deserted as the alley. The CLOSED sign hung on the front door beneath yellow strips with strange pictures and words in red ink. But that was deceptive, for deep within the basement, the tiger wizard, Mr. Hu, was debating strategy with the Lady Torka, who was in charge of the defenders. She had taken her true form, of a fox with a beautiful pair of snowy white wings. The feathers were tipped with edged steel so that they looked like rows of daggers. Around one foreleg was a cloth band with a headless

1

snake, the emblem of the rebels.

"Everything is ready," the tiger said, his voice echoing in the huge chamber that had been created just last month beneath his store. He sat upon one of the many cushioned benches. "The dragon mages have created the portal charms and we are placing them around Chinatown. The dragons will come when we send word."

Lady Torka accepted a cup of tea from Tom, the boy who was Mr. Hu's apprentice. She seemed too dainty to have led a group of rebels against their terrible master, Vatten, and to now face dreadful punishments if captured.

She tapped her folded white fan against her chin. "The dragons take a risk in coming here when their own kingdom is under attack," Lady Torka warned.

"His Highness knows the risk, but the stakes are worth it," Mr. Hu said as he took the other cup from his apprentice.

"If only we can make this happen." Lady Torka's frustrated sigh sent the steam whirling about over her cup. "So far, Vatten has had the initiative. He strikes where and when he wants but never with his whole strength. It is like fighting a will-o'-the-wisp. We need to lure all of Vatten's forces into the open so we can crush them."

"We have to draw him into a trap somehow," Mr. Hu agreed.

For ages in China, Vatten had been seeking the fabled phoenix, who had the power to change people's wills, either for good or evil. A past Guardian had fled to America with the phoenix egg, where it had passed into the hands of succeeding Guardians, including Tom's grandmother and now Mr. Hu.

Mr. Hu had managed to create an alliance of Lady Torka's rebels, who had once served Vatten, the dragons, and a force of heroes and spirits from China. It was the crowning achievement, so far, of Mr. Hu's brief Guardianship to bring together these former foes, united by their hatred of Vatten and their desire to keep the phoenix from the mad monster's control.

When Vatten's spies had stolen the phoenix egg, Tom and Mr. Hu had both nearly died recovering it. They had retreated to the dragon kingdom, where the dragons, desperate to fight off Vatten's followers, had stolen the egg for themselves and forced the phoenix to hatch prematurely.

With the birth of the phoenix, old powers stirred from their slumbers to wreak havoc again; and for the last month, the world had gone to war—though few humans knew it. Around the world, in the wilds of the land and sea, fantastical armies drew themselves up into ranks and fought fiercely, with no mercy being asked or given, as Vatten's followers sought to reach the phoenix and the allies tried to prevent them.

However, the deadliest and greatest battle was currently being waged in San Francisco's Chinatown. Friend and foe operated in small units, hunting and being hunted. Struggles broke out in alleys, on rooftops, and within the sewers, and were as vicious as they were brief, ending before the police arrived, with all the casualties removed. As yet, neither side wanted human interference in their shadow war. The television and newspapers blamed any destruction on gang warfare; and even though the human gangs insisted they were not at fault, no one believed them.

Tom nearly dropped the tray when he heard the screech. Shrill and angry, the sound ripped through a roof and two floors and into the subterranean chamber. Tom couldn't help trembling, which made the tea pot rattle.

Tom wondered what dreadful monster was trying to break into the store now. He'd already fought some creatures straight out of his nightmares—and a few so awful he could never have imagined them.

Even the battle-hardened Lady Torka glanced upward anxiously. "Are you sure the phoenix is safe here?"

"The store was a former bank, so it's strong structurally, and it's on the nexus of several lines of ch'i. My wards have made it into a fortress against most magic," Mr. Hu said. He took the tray with the Spode teapot from his nervous apprentice and set it down on the bench. "And I trust your warriors." As if on cue, the screeching ended abruptly as the defenders dealt with the threat.

With each passing day, the store felt more and more like a prison and everyone's nerves became frayed by the daily assaults. Tom found himself prowling about the store almost as much as the tiger did.

Lady Torka rose. "Still, I should see what's happened. Thank you for the tea. It was quite delicious," she said, as calmly as if she were leaving to tend her garden.

Mr. Hu sprang from the couch and bowed. "As you see fit, Lady Torka. Only a fool would argue with your wisdom."

"Take good care of our phoenix, Thomas." Lady Torka saluted him with her fan. Her eyes lingered on the golden scale on Tom's cheek.

When Tom had lain dying, his desperate master had sought the help of the strange and whimsical Empress Nü Kua. (Wise folk never even mentioned her name but referred to her simply as the Empress.) She had a reputation for granting wishes in her own quirky and sometimes cruel way, and she had done just that. After restoring Tom's strength, she had left the golden scale on his cheek, saying that he could use it to summon her. From everything he had heard about her, Tom hoped that day would never come.

At the meeting that formed the Alliance, Tom had found himself receiving a level of attention and respect unusual for an apprentice—due to what his master referred to as "the mark of the Empress's favor." Others, though, seemed to think of it as more of a curse and had been careful to keep their distance from him.

Tom was not sure what to say, so Mr. Hu spoke up for his apprentice. "He will do his duty, as shall we all." With another polite bow, the tiger escorted the lady out of the chamber and up the stairs to the apartment that led out to the store.

Glancing about the alley to make sure it was clear of monsters, Mr. Hu lifted the ward from the front door and opened it.

Lady Torka transformed herself into a tiny woman with short red hair and a matching red velvet jumpsuit. Her wings became a long, white, silver-hemmed cloak that covered her like a bell. It swirled dramatically as she strode outside.

"Let us hope we succeed," Mr. Hu muttered as he locked the door and again posted the ward.

The worried look on Mr. Hu's face when he returned downstairs made Tom feel even more uneasy. "We're going to win, aren't we?"

Mr. Hu roused himself from his dark thoughts. "Strategy isn't for apprentices to discuss." The tiger wagged a claw. "You're just trying to get out of doing your homework."

"The spell keeps coming out in reverse." Tom shrugged. "I freeze the eggplant instead of cooking it."

"That eggplant is supposed to be our dinner." Mr. Hu's whiskers twitched. "We covered this enchantment thoroughly yesterday. You seemed to know it then."

"I know that spell inside and out," Tom said. "I'm not sure what's going wrong. Anyway, shouldn't I be learning how to blast monsters instead of how to cook dinner?"

Mr. Hu reared upward on the tips of his hind paws. "The fire spell is far trickier than the wind spell you've mastered. It has far more parts and a much more complicated order, so you must master it on a small scale first."

The tiger turned everything into a magic lesson. Sometimes Tom suspected it was just a way of getting him to do chores. Then, guiltily, he reminded himself that he had a good deal to learn and little time to do it.

Mr. Hu clasped his paws behind his back. "Why don't you try while I observe you."

Embarrassed, Tom walked through the apartment, making excuses. "I don't seem to be able to control it. The Grand Mage said it might be my tiger's blood that makes my magic go wild."

While Mr. Hu had been recovering in the dragon kingdom, the greatest of the dragon wizards had tutored Tom; but to the tiger's dismay, he had learned dragon magic rather than the Lore of the Guardians. So Mr. Hu was determined that they make up for lost time. Tom spent almost every waking moment practicing some part of the Lore.

"Ha! The magic of tigers is far superior to that of the dragons." Mr. Hu's tail lashed back and forth with such indignation, he knocked over a chair. "Tiger magic will give you a power that any dragon would envy."

"Why is tiger magic so strong?" Tom asked.

The Guardian tapped his forehead. "Dragon magic comes from up here, but tiger magic comes from here." He touched his chest. "Tiger magic is the magic of Nature itself, and that makes it even harder to tame."

When they entered the kitchen, Mr. Hu's thick eyebrows rose and his ears wriggled as he saw the garbage can full of Tom's previous failures; but before he could lecture his apprentice, the cause of the war skittered in.

"Mama, Mama," cried the little red ball of fluff. "Read book!"

For the thousandth time, Tom tried to correct the phoenix. "I'm just the apprentice. Talk to him. He's the one in charge." He pointed at Mr. Hu.

Mr. Hu gave a sniff. "If the phoenix had seen me first when the egg hatched, things might be different. But instead he saw you, Master Thomas. Like many birds, he thinks the first creature he sees is his mother. It is called imprinting, as you know."

"In other words, you're stuck," Räv said from the doorway of her bedroom.

Tom could feel his tiger's blood rushing through his face so that his cheeks became beet red and his head felt like a teakettle that was boiling. But before he could open his mouth, Mr. Hu clapped a paw over it. "Mind your manners, Master Thomas," the tiger warned. "Mistress Räv is our guest and a representative of her people."

"The official ambassador," Räv corrected. She plucked at her rebel armband. "And Lady Torka's personal choice."

Not for the first time, Tom wondered if her new title had gone to the girl's head. He forced himself to take several slow, deep breaths. When the tiger dropped his paw, Tom mumbled, "Sorry. It's hard to keep my temper these days."

This had been an unfortunate—or in Mr. Hu's opinion, a fortunate—side effect when the Guardian had shared part of his soul with Tom: Not only had his hair become streaked and his eyes flecked with amber, but Tom's temper had become as violent as a tiger's.

"I found mastering my temper was even harder than thaumaturgical calculus," Mr. Hu sympathized, "but somehow you'll have to, just as I'm still learning to. Do you think it's easy for me to remain inside here like prey? I would much rather be outside, fighting like Monkey and Mistral." He squinted at the girl, noticing for the first time the precious garment she wore. "Where did you get that robe?"

"I found it in a trunk upstairs." She stroked the antique blue-and-silver robe, luxuriating in the feel of the silk. "As the official ambassador—"

The tiger held up his paw indulgently. "Yes, yes. We'll

consider it a loan, then; but I want it back in the same condition when you're done. It's a valuable antique from the Sung dynasty."

"I'll treat it like it was my own," Räv promised. She had once been Vatten's spy and had helped her lord steal the egg and draw Mr. Hu and Tom into a deadly trap— only to find herself abandoned to die with them. She had been shocked when the Guardian had included her in their escape, and she had been devoted to him ever since.

"Read book, Mama!" the phoenix demanded as he began to climb Tom's pant leg. Though the hatchling was only a month old, he was developing fast and already had the maturity, if not the size, of a two-year-old human child.

"Not now," Tom said as he felt the tiny claws. "I've got my homework to do."

"No, you read, Mama," the bored phoenix cheeped as it climbed up his chest and managed to reach his shoulder.

"Later," Tom said as he placed an eggplant in the pan for yet another try. He squirmed resentfully as the little bird treated him like a personal jungle gym. He seemed to spend half the day taking care of the phoenix and the other half studying the Lore. It hadn't been much of a summer.

"Read, Mama. Read."

"Get off me," Tom growled as he tried to consult Ko

Hung's *The Magical Kitchen.*

"Read, read, read," the phoenix chanted as he danced upon Tom's head.

"I've got to concentrate," Tom said as he tried to snatch the bird.

"I wouldn't let Junior get too excited, if I were you," Räv advised.

"Don't you have ambassadoring to do?"

The silver-haired girl grinned at Tom as she crossed her arms. "This is better than television."

The excited phoenix plopped down on Tom's head as if it were a soft beanbag, and the bird's feet became entangled in his tiger-striped hair. Even then, the phoenix kept on insisting that his "mother" read him a story.

Tom started to squirm, but it was too late. The wetness told him the bird had had yet another accident. "He's supposed to be the King of all the Birds; he ought to be housebroken at least," Tom snarled. Closing his eyes, he counted to ten, trying to stay calm.

"Even kings and queens start out as babies, and babies do what comes naturally," Mr. Hu replied. "But perhaps, Mistress Räv, you'll kindly read to the phoenix while Master Thomas sees to our dinner."

However much she might tease Mr. Hu, Räv would do anything he asked. Sitting on the floor, she patted her knee. "Come on, Junior. I'll read to you since Mama's real tiger-ish today."

"Don't you start on me too. I'm trying to control it," Tom grumbled as he reached for the bird perched on his head.

"Not that one," the phoenix said when Räv took a book from the top of a pile. "I want good one."

"Good one, good one." Räv scratched her cheek with the book as she stared at the stack. "Which one is that?"

"His favorite is that book about the family going to a picnic," Tom said, groaning inwardly. He had lost count of how many times he had read it to the bird.

"Oh, that one," Räv said, making a face. "Talk about make-believe." But she dug around in the stack until she found it.

Tom's hands groped for the phoenix. He had gently disentangled the bird when he suddenly felt a sharp nip. "Ow!"

When he lowered the phoenix, he would have sworn the bird was smiling mischievously.

He felt his tiger's temper rising but fought it down. "Bad phoenix, bad phoenix," he scolded as he deposited the feathery ball in Räv's lap. "No hurt Mama!"

Tom felt a twinge of guilt as the bird lowered his head until his beak was resting on Räv's knee. The chick always looked so sad when he couldn't feel Tom's warmth. "Yes, Mama."

Tom cleaned his hair as best he could with a paper towel and then washed his hands. "You said the phoenix was supposed to be peaceful, but all he does is make trouble."

"Master Thomas, you must be as patient with the phoenix as I must be with you. He has the potential for good but it is not automatic." The elderly tiger looked down his muzzle at Tom. "Like any child, he must be taught the difference between right and wrong so that when he comes into his full powers he can make wise decisions. That is your task, as it is mine to teach you."

"So Tom gets to roar and show his fangs a lot, like you do with him?" Räv asked impishly.

Mr. Hu's whiskers twitched as he fought his own battle to control his temper. "I have taught Master Thomas far more than that, Mistress Räv. With my help, he's mastered his wind spell."

"Yes," Tom said, "but I've learned more about sweeping and dusting than I have about magic. At least you ought to get a vacuum cleaner."

Mr. Hu's nostrils widened as he took a deep breath and let it out. "The old ways are the best. Brooms build—"

"Character." Tom moaned as he rolled his eyes.

"Exactly," Mr. Hu said, unable to resist smiling. "Now, why don't you begin."

Tom started to murmur, his hands moving in an intricate pattern, as he tried to ignore Räv reading about the family of a grandfather, an uncle, an aunt, and a pet dog that went on a picnic. The little bird wriggled happily when Räv pointed to him and said he was like "baby" in the book.

Shutting out everything at last, Tom unleashed the spell upon the hapless eggplant in the pan on top of the stove. Then he straightened, hoping to smell it roasting, but its deep violet skin was dusted with ice crystals.

Cautiously, he poked the purple side. "It's frozen solid again." His lip curled instinctively in a snarl. Resisting the impulse to smash the eggplant with his fist, he forced himself to count to ten instead.

Räv did not help when she tapped a picture in the book and asked, "And where's Mama?"

"There," the phoenix said, waving a wingtip at Tom.

"Don't encourage him," Tom said as he dumped his latest mistake into the garbage can with its unfortunate predecessors.

"But where Papa?" the phoenix demanded.

Räv looked at Tom impishly. "Yeah, where's Papa?"

"How do I know?" he growled, exasperated.

At that moment, Sidney, another of their friends, flew into the kitchen with a humming noise. The fur on the rat's back vibrated, so that he resembled a fuzzy yellow balloon. "There you are, Mr. H.," he scolded, waving a blueprint in one paw with several more tucked under a foreleg. "You said you'd check the additions after you finished with Lady Torka."

The bird hesitated and then indicated the hovering rat

14

uncertainly. "Is that Papa?"

"Gee, sorry, kid, but nope," the rat said.

"I want Papa." The phoenix pointed a wingtip at Mr. Hu. "Is that him?"

"Absolutely not." The tiger bristled.

Sidney hovered in front of the Guardian's head. "Now, about that home theater."

Mr. Hu's ears flattened tight against his head as he growled. "For the hundredth time, I do not want one. Nor do I want a sauna. Nor do I desire a stable."

The yellow rat buzzed about, unperturbed by the exposed fangs. "It's cheaper to add them now."

The beleaguered tiger whirled around and crouched, tail lashing at the air. "Sidney, I only authorized a chamber big enough for the meeting, and you did that already!"

"Tell you what. We'll put in the conduits for wiring so they'll be easy to add later." The rat thrust the load of blueprints into Mr. Hu's paws. "Hold these, will you, while I make a note?"

The surprised tiger tried to balance the blueprints. "I don't want any additions. I order you to cease and desist!"

Sidney's fur flattened, and he settled down on the floor. The rat took a notebook and pencil out from under his small yellow hard hat. "I also found a list of stuff that's not up to code. Some contractor cheated when he built this dump."

Something large crashed against the roof, causing the

15

entire building to shudder and bits of plaster to fall from the ceiling. Tom couldn't help cringing but forced himself to straighten up.

The phoenix tilted his head back to stare upward. "Mama, what that?"

"Remember, Master Thomas, Mistress Räv," Mr. Hu said quietly. "We must create as safe and happy a life as we can for the phoenix so that he will grow up healthy in mind as well as in body."

Though his hand was shaking, Tom tried to keep his voice as calm as he could while he dusted off the little bird. "It's nothing."

"Oh," the phoenix said.

Poor thing, Tom thought, he must assume that everyone lived in a home under siege.

"We'll need to . . . replaster too," Sidney continued as he made a note about the hole that had just appeared on the kitchen ceiling.

Suddenly the lights went out.

"Mama, Mama!" the phoenix cried in alarm.

"Everything's okay," Tom reassured the little bird as he groped for the matches and candles. Emergencies like this were happening all too often. "It's just Sidney's lousy wiring."

"Hey," the rat's voice called indignantly from the blackness, "everything I did is up to code. It's not my fault. It's— Ow!"

16

When Tom struck the match, he saw that Mr. Hu had stepped on Sidney's tail. "Everything's perfectly normal, so what else could it be, Sidney?" Tom said menacingly and jerked his head toward the phoenix.

"Yeah, I guess it is," Sidney muttered, pulling his injured tail from beneath the tiger's paw. "I'll check on it."

As Tom lit a candle, they could hear sounds of a vicious fight taking place up above. When he saw the trembling bird had retreated to his nest, a box filled with shredded paper, Tom forced himself to forget his own fears. Picking up the phoenix, he set the chick on his shoulder.

The phoenix tugged at Tom's ear with his beak. "Hungry, Mama."

Tom used his candle to light the others. "I still haven't got that fire spell down yet, so you'll have to wait until we get the power back and I can use the stove."

The phoenix began to hop up and down on his shoulder. "Hungry now."

"You can't always get your way." Tom was trying his best to keep control of his temper; but it was hard when everyone, including this walking feather duster, treated him like a servant. "You'll eat as soon as— Ow!" he cried when the phoenix pecked his cheek.

"Mama, Mama," the phoenix peeped. "Hungry now, now, now!"

When Tom swiveled his head, the ball of red fluff

17

seemed to fill his eyes. "What can I do if we don't have electricity? Quit pestering me."

The phoenix's feathers frizzed outward as if he had been struck by lightning. "I no pest. Hungry, hungry!" He pecked Tom's cheek again.

"Ow!" Tom said, and snatched the phoenix away from his face. "Will you quit that? Boy, am I ever glad there's only one of you."

The phoenix's eyes were as shiny as wet pebbles. "Not only one." He pouted. "You Mama."

"Will you get it into your feather brain? I can't be your mother!"

The phoenix tilted his head to the side. "Only one?"

"That's right," Tom growled. "And thank heaven for that, because one is enough to handle."

Two tiny tears appeared in the phoenix's eyes and slid across the soft downy cheeks. "No Mama? No family? Only one?"

"You got Mama all wrong." Getting to her feet, Räv petted the little bird's head. "He meant you're special."

Mr. Hu shot a terrifying look at his apprentice. "That's right. You're unique," the tiger said.

But the tears were streaming from the phoenix's eyes now, dampening its face so that it turned a deep crimson. "No one."

"Okay, okay, I'll feed you," Tom said exasperatedly.

"Feed myself," the phoenix said defiantly.

"Yeah, right," Tom mumbled as he set the bird down on the floor.

"He is only a month old, Master Thomas," Mr. Hu reminded him.

Before Tom could answer, they heard a thud from the alley and a moment later there was a knocking at the front door.

"I doubt if Vatten's monsters have suddenly discovered their manners," Mr. Hu said. "Master Thomas, see who it is, but don't admit them unless they give the proper signal."

Holding his candle before him, Tom left the apartment and entered the store in front. Monkey was leaning wearily against the doorway. To hide his true identity from Vatten's spies, he was disguised as a little man with curly brown hair and sideburns, wearing a white jogging suit and a fake leopard-skin cap. His clothes were ripped in several places, and though he did his best to smile, he looked tired.

Mistral stood behind him; the dragon was disguised as an elegant woman in a shimmering black suit, but there were bags under her eyes as well.

After Monkey tapped out the signal to ensure it truly was him, Tom removed the ward from the door and opened it.

"The pigeons are getting bigger and bigger this year." Monkey gestured with his thumb at a scaled tail that was disappearing back onto the rooftops. "Our friends are carting away any embarrassing 'details.'"

"I trust you didn't come back just so you could brag," Mr. Hu said from the doorway of the apartment. "Did you finish putting up the dragons' charms?"

"Yep," Monkey said, shuffling inside without his usual energy.

Mistral followed him into the store. "I wouldn't mind some lunch. Fighting always gives me such an appetite."

When he thought of how Mistral and Monkey were risking their lives, Tom felt guilty for complaining about his chores. "I'll forget the magic for now and just get everyone else's meal together somehow after I take care of the phoenix," he said, and returned to the kitchen where he had left the bird.

The lights flickered into life, but the phoenix was gone.

CHAPTER TWO

The Fisher Folk

They have fished for many generations but prefer using their hands
to anything else. Over the ages, these people have developed long
arms to catch fish.

—Shan Hai Ching

Monkey looked down at his feet in dismay. "I didn't see anything pass."

"But we weren't watching for anyone that small," Mistral said, twisting her head from left to right. "All our efforts have come undone in a moment's carelessness."

"No time for moaning," Mr. Hu cut in. "We should split up and search. Sidney, you cover the financial district to the east." The rat knew that area well from when he ran a messenger service. "Monkey, you take the hotels in the west. I'll take North Beach." That was the Italian area. "Mistral, take the south." The dragon would cover the fancy stores and restaurants.

"What about us?" Räv objected.

"It's much too dangerous," Mr. Hu insisted. "And someone needs to remain behind in the store."

"So let Tom stay. I can take care of myself," Räv said.

"The same here," Tom chimed in. He wasn't about to stay in the store when it was his fault the phoenix was lost. "You need every searcher you can get. And he trusts me." He touched the pouch around his neck, which contained the charm Mr. Hu had given him when he first became the tiger's apprentice. "I have this to protect me."

Mr. Hu's chin sank to his chest as he thought for a moment. "Very well. But remember, Master Thomas, your charm will aid you against the lesser monsters but not against the more powerful ones." He regarded each of the children in turn. "It would be best to avoid them all: Skill with a knife and mastery of a solitary spell make neither a warrior nor a wizard. If you find Vatten's followers have already captured the phoenix, don't try to get him back yourself. Get help."

Mistral arched an eyebrow. "Is that wise to send the children off alone?"

"During a war, there's no time for children to be children." Mr. Hu sighed. "Sidney and Mistress Räv will switch. Sidney, stay here and be sure to put up the wards after us. Master Thomas, search Grant Avenue. Mistress Räv, take the east." That was where big companies had their skyscrapers.

Monkey glanced this way and that, but no one was around. "I'll tell our guards to start searching too."

Mr. Hu reminded the ape before he left. "Discreetly.

22

We don't want to alert Vatten's spies that the phoenix is loose and vulnerable." The tiger assumed his own human disguise to hide his identity.

"The alley should be safe at least," Mistral said when they were all outside.

"But beyond that it could be dangerous." Mr. Hu wagged a finger at the children. "And I repeat: Do nothing reckless."

"I've been taking care of myself for years on the streets," Räv said confidently.

The boy stuck up for himself as well. "And I helped beat the Nameless One," Tom said. That had been a giant monster that had terrorized the dragon kingdom until he and Mistral had destroyed it.

The Guardian's forehead wrinkled with concern. "Overconfidence is as deadly as any monster."

"Hu!" Mistral called, impatient to be off.

"Yes, yes." With one last, worried look, the tiger headed off with Mistral. Despite their bold words, the children lingered at the mouth of the alley. They had not been this far outside since the war for the phoenix had begun. From the corner of his eye, Tom noticed the edge of a poster flapping up to reveal one of the dragon's charms hidden beneath it, the handiwork of Monkey and Mistral. Quickly he smoothed it down, and the glue held.

Then he turned his attention to the passersby on Grant Avenue. A dozen shoppers bustled by with plastic bags of groceries; and a pair of tourists, shivering in T-shirts and shorts in San Francisco's usual summer weather, hurried along in the crowd. He scanned each intently, wondering if any were a friend or an enemy in disguise.

Räv brushed past Tom to begin her search of Chinatown's main thoroughfare. "We'll never find the phoenix, standing here."

Taking a breath, Tom followed her into the war zone. When a man jumped out of the back of a delivery truck parked partway on the sidewalk, Tom paused warily. Though he didn't feel the telltale tingling at the back of his neck that would indicate magic, he muttered a quick spell to confirm this—but the man was just a truck driver loading boxes.

As Tom continued on alone, he passed a little bakery shop. Through the plate glass window, he saw two old men sitting inside. Were either of them Vatten's spies? Again he worked the revelation spell, but all he saw were elderly folk intent on nursing their Styrofoam cups of tea while they gossiped.

Tom eyed a trio of determined tourists who were snapping pictures of huge ten-gallon drums of MSG. He used the spell again but they were normal as well.

And then he realized that if he checked whether everyone he passed was a disguised monster, it would take him an hour to go one block. He would just have to chance it.

His stomach twisting tight as a cord, Tom hurried along the sidewalk. At least he had his wind spell to use as a weapon. What protection did the newly hatched phoenix have against monsters?

Tom told himself that the chick couldn't help being a nuisance. There were many times when Tom wished other people had more patience when he made a mistake; and now he saw that he was just as bad.

Whenever his grandmother had defended Tom to his principal after one of his many fights at school, she would say that frightened boys did stupid things. Perhaps the phoenix was like his "mama" after all, in this regard, and needed to be taught not to strike out in fear. Tom just hoped the phoenix would be a better pupil than he had been.

Tom had reached the intersection when he heard someone yowl, "Help! Murder! Demons!"

Had Vatten's monsters struck? Hoping his wind spell would be enough to defend himself, Tom spun around, plunging up a side street until he came to a plump storekeeper standing outside his store and brandishing a broom.

From the outside, it was not clear what the store sold, but there was nothing that would have attracted a tourist. In the narrow window were magazines with fading photographs of Chinese movie and musical stars, along with ugly plastic dolls in Chinese jackets and pants, and a faded cardboard sign for Lion Salve. Amber necklaces were draped around a Buddha's neck, but he felt no tingling, so they must have been harmless lumps from the Baltic Sea. Mr. Hu had told him there were some magical pieces of amber that were the souls of dead tigers.

"What happened?" Tom was panting from the uphill run.

The storekeeper seemed glad to have an audience for his grievances. "This . . . this demon came in and wrecked my altar." He jabbed his broom at the inside of the store.

Tom saw a small table overturned in a corner of the dark interior; a tiny altar lay on its side. Tea puddling around a broken cup had extinguished the still-smoking candles, and oranges were scattered on the floor. One orange had been half-pecked.

"And then that little monster almost started a fire when the candlesticks fell over," the owner complained.

The store was so packed that Tom thought it was a small miracle the overturned candles hadn't done some damage.

Tom found himself hoping that it was one of Vatten's spies, rather than the phoenix, who had caused this damage. "What did the monster look like?" he asked.

"It came and went so fast, I'm not sure; but it looked like a small feather duster," the owner said.

Tom swallowed guiltily. "Was it red?"

The owner lowered his broom. "Is it yours?" he asked suspiciously.

"Not really." Tom gulped. As he rushed away, he couldn't help blaming himself. If he hadn't hurt the little bird's feelings, the chick might not have wandered off. Even when he had lost his grandmother, the only human he'd loved after his parents disappeared, Tom had known there were others of his kind. He could only guess at how lonely the phoenix must feel.

A half block away, Tom almost bumped into a man and a woman arguing heatedly by a fruit stand. The woman was cradling a small dog in her arms. "My Gertie would never bite anyone."

The man was doing a good imitation of a stork, standing on one leg so he could massage the ankle of the other. "Well, something got me."

"And something nipped my bag." Another woman was holding her plastic bag in both arms so everyone could see the hole. A line of fallen mushrooms marked her path. A man with arms long enough to be a professional basketball player was helping her pick them up. He watched curiously as Tom hurried by, following the trail of destruction up the street.

The phoenix must be starving, searching for some food. Tom gave a start. He was starting to think like the phoenix's real mother would!

It was easy to follow the phoenix's trail now, for the bird had left various wreckage in his wake. Plastic bags from the stores lay shredded on the street. T-shirts had been trampled by panicked people. The phoenix was having a royal temper tantrum.

Tom bit his lip. It was just as Mr. Hu had said: The phoenix had the same potential for good or evil as any creature. And from the malicious destruction the little bird had left, the phoenix definitely had to be steered away from his bad side. Even though part of Tom resented the pesky creature, the stronger part of him felt sorry for the phoenix. He was so small and fragile, perhaps he had struck as much from frustration as from mischief.

Suddenly Tom heard a plaintive, "Mama, Mama."

His tiger's blood racing through his veins, Tom bounded down an alley and out onto a steep street. The sound came from in front of a delicatessen.

"Mama, Mama," the phoenix cried shrilly as he huddled beneath the ducks, stripped of their feathers, that dangled like pale footballs in the window.

The bundle of red fluff seemed so helpless at that moment. Tom could feel the bird shivering as he cupped the hatchling between his palms. "Shh, it's okay. I'm here."

The phoenix's legs twitched as he tried to balance. "Mama?" he asked in a small, uncertain voice.

Tom felt his cheeks reddening but he couldn't deny

the relief he felt. "I'm here."

The phoenix trembled as he stared up at the ducks.

"Those are ducks. People don't harm phoenixes," Tom quickly assured him.

"Bad, bad, bad!" The phoenix leaped from his hands and began to scamper toward the store's doorway, hunting the killer. "I hurt you! I hurt you!"

Tom knew he had to guide the phoenix. The hatchling was enjoying the thought of revenge.

"No," Tom snarled. "No hurt."

The phoenix paused and stared up at him, so worshipful and curious. "No hurt?"

His trust filled Tom with wonder. No one had ever depended on him like this before, and it made him feel both warm and frightened. But it was a different sort of fear: He was afraid to fail the faith that the little bird seemed to have in him. Was this how Mr. Hu felt when he taught Tom?

"No," Tom growled, shaking his head for emphasis as the tiny bird drank in his every word. "No hurt anyone."

"Mama says?" the phoenix asked meekly.

"Mama says," Tom insisted. Licking a finger, he began to clean up the little bird, who submitted patiently.

When Tom was done, the phoenix jumped onto his arm. "We go home?"

Tom felt a strange thrill as the little bird slipped under his sleeve and began to tickle him as it climbed up his arm. Would a real parent feel that way? Anyway, what was so wrong about creating your own family? Mr. Hu had become his family after his grandmother died, and so had their other friends.

"You're awfully dumb, you know that?" Tom said when the phoenix emerged from his open collar and began to nuzzle his cheek lovingly. "But I guess that makes me even dumber."

Tom hurried down the hill, past the dark buildings. He jumped when the bird broke the silence. "Pretty, pretty!"

The phoenix was gazing raptly at a crystal star that hung by a thin nylon string in the window of a souvenir store. The narrow street was gloomy with shadows except for a brief space where the sun beamed between the crowded buildings. But now the star seemed to absorb that light, bursting into life with tips that glittered like silvery fire and a rainbow within. It seemed almost as if a diamond had blossomed with iridescent petals.

"Ooo, pretty, pretty," the phoenix peeped.

"Yes, it is," Tom said absently, eager to get back to safety.

The phoenix struggled to get to the star. "Mine."

He had to distract the bird somehow. Desperate, Tom opened his shirt and tucked the phoenix inside the pouch that held the protective charm.

"Pretty, pretty!" As the bird fought to see the star, his claws tickled Tom's chest.

"Stop that," Tom said, giggling. "Now stay there." He

pressed the bird close to him.

The phoenix obeyed for all of five seconds before he began squirming again. "Can't see," he complained.

So they had to compromise by letting him peek out of Tom's shirt between two buttons.

"Pretty, mine," the phoenix breathed in awe.

"Some other day," Tom said, turning impatiently.

"No go," the phoenix said. Tom felt it peck him.

"If you do that again, I'll never buy it for you," Tom warned as he continued to walk on.

The phoenix sulked for about a block before it said, "Boom, boom, boom."

"That's my heart," Tom said, making a guess.

"Mama," the phoenix said, snuggling closer.

Tom had never had this effect on anyone. The phoenix really did need him.

Deciding that he should take the phoenix back to the store as quickly as possible, he took a shortcut down an alley. Cut off from the light, the deserted lane lay in a perpetual twilight. His footsteps echoed against the brick walls. He was halfway down the alley when he heard a scurrying sound from above.

The phoenix pulled his head into the pouch. "Scary."

"I won't let anyone hurt you," Tom promised. He stared toward the rooftops but there was nothing but sky. Picking up his pace, he hurried along; but he could not shake the feeling that he was being followed and he broke into a trot, keeping one hand along the rough bricks to guide him.

He thought he saw a long, long pole reaching down from a rooftop; but then his neck began to tingle and he realized the "pole" was a long arm, ending in a hand. On the back of the wrist was a violet tattoo of a 9 with a serpent's coiled tail. It was the symbol of Vatten's followers. They had found him.

Leathery fingers, long and slender as melting candles, groped toward him. Tom covered the phoenix with one hand. "Go away. He's mine!" he roared, and realized that he meant it.

"He's Lord Vatten's!" the thief cried defiantly from above. The fingers were as agile as hummingbirds as they grabbed Tom's wrist—and then jerked back as if they had grabbed a live electric wire. Far overhead, the thief whined in pain from Tom's protective charm.

The phoenix had emerged from his pouch to snap at the thief's hand. "No hurt Mama."

Tom had come to save the phoenix; but it was the little bird that wanted to protect him now. He felt something catch in his throat.

Another hand, ignoring the shock, seized him, and before he could mutter his wind spell a hand covered his mouth.

The blood was pounding in his head as he bit the hand covering his mouth. It tasted of dirt and fish, but he had the satisfaction of hearing a howl of pain and the hand vanished upward. Then his teeth sank into the other hand clutching him and that one flashed upward also.

"Mama bites someone," the phoenix said in shock as it peeked out of the pouch.

"It's all right if Mama does it," Tom said lamely, feeling as inept as the awful school counselors who had tried to get him to stop fighting.

Around him, more arms, thin as pipes but long as street lamps, arched down. The strange fingers looked like roots that were growing out of the very air itself. Perhaps the earlier man with long arms he had seen on the street had been their scout?

There was no time to cast spells. Crouching and dodging from side to side, Tom had almost reached the mouth of the alley when one hand managed to snag his sleeve and another grabbed his collar. Then a third snagged his ear. Before he could blink, his body and head were seized by dozens of hands and his mouth was covered. Moving in any direction, let alone doing magic, was now impossible.

"No hurt Mama!" the phoenix shouted.

Desperate as any tiger wanting to protect his cub, Tom sank his teeth again into the hand over his mouth and heard a howl of pain; but the thief resolutely kept his hand in place this time.

Helplessly, he could only watch as more hands reached for the little bird. He twisted and wriggled frantically, but he could not pull free. Even his roars of frustration were muffled through the thief's fingers.

"I knew you'd get in trouble without me. Like Mama, like son."

By some miracle Räv lounged at the exit to the alley, the hem of the antique robe hitched up around her knees so she could move faster.

He hardly dared to believe his eyes. He moved the only thing he could, his eyebrows, trying somehow to tell her to find Mr. Hu.

He could see the silver-haired girl understood, but she curled her lips contemptuously. "I don't need help to deal with Fishers." And she slipped the stiletto blade from her sleeve. "I can handle this."

What could one person do against that forest of arms? Tom twitched his eyebrows frantically.

But Räv was already moving toward him, and there was a look in her eyes as wild as when she had fought with them on the rooftops. It seemed as if this outcast girl did not care if she lived or died so long as she could repay the Guardian's kindness. Her steps quickened until she was charging, slashing fearlessly at the hands that tried to stop her.

Howls of pain erupted as the thieves yanked their injured fingers away. When some of his captors pulled away to halt his rescuer, Tom wrenched himself free.

Hoping that Mr. Hu was right about the power of tiger

magic, he lifted his hands and summoned the wind spell. The blast of air knocked the remaining arms aside as if they were straw, and they scraped against the walls as more howls rained from the roof.

"Thanks," Tom said as he headed over to Räv.

"I told you I didn't need anyone to take care of me," she panted as she sliced at a thief. Her robe was already torn in several places, with one sleeve missing, and her hair was all tangled. "But I might have underestimated them a tiny bit, so"—she slashed at another hand—"let's get out of here."

That was easier said than done, for the determined thieves reached with bruised, bleeding hands to grab them; and it wasn't long before they were both held in a web of arms and hands once again. While Tom did his best to protect the frightened phoenix in his pouch, Räv twisted desperately, trying to escape.

Then from up above, Tom heard Monkey say, "Don't you know it's not nice to steal?"

There was a chorus of frightened yelps and then Mistral was giving the battle cry of her tribe: "Kamsin! Kamsin!"

The next moment, the arms had vanished, dropping Tom and Räv on the ground. High overhead, Tom could hear the sounds of a battle upon the rooftop.

Slowly he lowered his hand from protecting the phoenix. "Are you all right?"

"Mama no hurt?" the phoenix asked.

"I'm just fine," Tom said as he sat up.

"Why they want me? Kill me like duck?" The phoenix shivered.

Tom petted the downy back, trying to calm him down. "No, they want you alive."

"Why?" the little bird demanded.

"I told you that you were special," Räv said, stowing her stiletto away in her remaining sleeve before she got up.

The phoenix's eyes widened. "I am? Really?"

"Remember, we told you there was only one of you," she said, unrolling the robe's hem so that it dropped once again around her legs. "Everyone wants you."

Exhausted, Tom slowly made his way toward the street. He didn't know how Mistral, Monkey, and the others handled the constant fighting. "Who were those thieves anyway?"

"The Fisher Folk," Räv said, trying to pull the edges of her torn robe together. "Their ancestors developed long arms to catch fish from the rivers and the seas. Some of them later turned to fishing for other people's belongings. And those thieves joined Vatten." She paused. "Look at these rips. What's Mr. Hu going to say?" She seemed more afraid of the Guardian than of their attackers.

Tom thought about the kind of life she might have led up until now. The few times he had tried to raise the subject, she had cut him off. Even sympathy seemed to make her uncomfortable.

"I'll help you sew it up," he said. "And thanks again."

"Yes, thanks," the phoenix echoed from inside Tom's shirt. "Thanks, Papa," he said, looking directly at the girl.

Räv's forehead wrinkled in a stern frown. "I'm not your papa."

The fluffy red head poked out of the pouch. "You Papa," the phoenix declared firmly, and then spread his wings to indicate both Räv and Tom. "We family."

"Stop that," Räv said and gave him a ferocious glower; but rather than frightening the bird, it only encouraged him.

"Papa, Papa, Papa," the phoenix repeated stubbornly.

The more she argued with the little bird, the more he insisted that she was his father.

"I could have told you it wouldn't work," Tom said with a grin, and could not resist adding, "Papa."

CHAPTER THREE

The Hao Pig

He resembles a small suckling pig and is covered with white quills as long as hairpins. The tips are black.

The Yen Huo

They are covered all over with black fur and cast fire from their mouths.

The P'ao Hsiao

The p'ao has a goat's body but a human's face and nails and a tiger's fangs. Its eyes are behind its front legs.

The Chu Chien

The chu chien have heads like humans' but their ears are like an ox's and they have only one eye. Their bodies resemble leopards with long tails and they have powerful roars.

The Jen-mien Hsiao

They have bodies like monkeys' and tails like dogs'. Their heads are shaped like owls' but with human faces.

—Shan Hai Ching

When they emerged from the alley, they saw Lady Torka walking briskly toward them. Despite her hurry, there was something almost dainty about her steps.

Waddling behind her were a dozen short-legged men in dark yellow leather whose white hair rose up in spikes tipped with black. Though they looked vaguely comical, Tom knew they were among the deadliest fighters in the shadow war. They were just a few steps ahead of the thick fog sweeping up the street like a gray tide. The mist had already consumed the tall towers that surrounded Chinatown and was quickly swallowing the buildings within as well.

"Lady Torka." Räv bowed to her and then to the leader of the men, whose hair was tipped with gold. "Lord Harnal. We've found the phoenix."

"Well done, Ambassador and Master Thomas," Lady Torka said, dipping her head first to Räv, then to Tom. "We'll escort you back to the Guardian's."

"And the sooner the better," Lord Harnal said uneasily, his small eyes surveying the fog. "How could the Guardian lose the phoenix at a time like this? This could lose the war for us! Maybe he's getting too old for his duties."

"We can place blame later," Lady Torka said pragmatically. "Master Yen is casting every spell he can to compel humans to seek shelter; and we'd best reach our own."

From his lessons, Tom had a sketchy idea of how those

spells worked—like a hypnotist's suggestions, the longing for home was planted in people's minds. It was simple enough magic, but it took a powerful wizard to do it on that kind of scale.

"This discussion isn't over," grumbled Lord Harnal as his gloved hand signed to his men to close around the children.

Räv looked at the mist that had wrapped around her ankles. "I think Master Yen could have spared us the fog, though. It'll slow us down."

"*This* isn't his." Lord Harnal kicked at the grayness that hid his feet. "It's all he can do to work his spells on so many humans. We don't want a lot of panicky civilians getting in our way."

Tom realized there was something odd about the mist; it left a cold, greasy feeling.

Lady Torka pressed her lips into a thin, grim line. "Both sides are preparing the battlefield." With a loud flap, she opened her fan, which was of carved bone and steel with sharp spikes. And Tom realized the fan was actually a deadly weapon, rather than a luxury.

"This is just the sort of mistake Vatten was waiting for," Lord Harnal said, and trotted into the fog. Though his legs were stubby, they were thick with muscle, and he set such a fast pace that the children had to jog to keep up with him.

"Stay out of sight," Tom whispered to the phoenix. He

saw two intelligent eyes move from within his shirt as the bird nodded. Tom was determined to protect the precious chick, his cub, with his life.

The fog seemed to grow thicker, so that even nearby buildings vanished. The only thing that existed was the small patch of road where Tom ran with the others. The mist against Tom's face had a metallic smell that made his tiger-sharpened nose wrinkle in disgust.

They had gone no more than fifty feet when a blue-faced woman in a furred top hat and coat blundered out of an alley. Tom recognized her as a fire-spitting *yen huo*.

Instantly, Lord Harnal and his Hao warriors transformed into huge pigs whose backs bristled with white quills, each as sharp as Räv's stiletto. And their gloved hands morphed into sharp trotters. Lady Torka changed into a fox with snow-white wings. Like her, the Hao wore rebel leg bands.

"Keep going," Lord Harnal shouted, and he nodded to one of his followers to take care of the threat.

The pig wheeled around, shouting, "Freedom!"—the battle cry of the rebels. He barely dodged the fire that shot from the yen huo's tubular mouth and then he went on the attack.

Lord Harnal and his men galloped on all fours now, quills clacking. Behind them, Tom saw light flash in the fog as flames burst from the yen huo's mouth.

"You mustn't stop or slow down, whatever happens,"

Lady Torka ordered Tom and Räv. "Our lives don't matter so long as you reach the Guardian's home with the phoenix. Until then, the whole world is at stake."

Abiding by her commands, they did not pause for the next monster who sprang out of a doorway. Or the one who leaped down from a rooftop. Instead, one of Lord Harnal's men peeled away from the group to deal with each new danger.

It became a nightmare dash through Chinatown. Tom never knew where the next monster was coming from—only that a paw with deadly claws or a hideous face with sharp fangs would suddenly stretch out from the mist; and they seemed to appear faster and faster. But his fear only made his tiger's blood pound through him harder, ready to strike down anything that threatened the phoenix.

However, as each new danger was met, their numbers dwindled until their only escorts consisted of Lord Harnal and Lady Torka.

"We've finally drawn out all of Vatten's scum," Lord Harnal panted.

"Good," Lady Torka said. "We can take advantage of it once we get the phoenix to safety."

"Ah," he grunted back. "One great battle in which we either sink or swim."

They were on Grant Avenue by then, a couple of blocks from the store. Tom was glad to see that the shops and restaurants had all closed and the street was deserted. Master Yen's spell appeared to have worked, and the humans had vanished into their homes.

Three men burst from the doorway of an apartment house. They had the spindliest arms and legs Tom had ever seen and their hair was tied up in ponytails on either side of their heads. Despite the cold, they were bare-chested. The next moment they had transformed into *p'ao*, goatlike creatures with human heads and horns. With triumphant wails, they exposed sharp fangs and threw themselves at the phoenix's defenders.

"Go on!" Lord Harnal yelled as he lowered his head and charged to meet them. The nimble pig seemed to be everywhere as he wheeled and thrust his tusks or stabbed with his quilled body.

The battle became a mass of whirling silhouettes. Lady Torka fixed on Räv. "You must see that the phoenix reaches safety."

"Yes, Lady," Räv said, clutching her stiletto tighter.

Lady Torka stared at Tom next. "And you must go on even if the ambassador stays to fight. Only the phoenix matters."

She had barely finished when they heard a new terror screeching toward them from above.

"Duck!" Lady Torka honked, spreading her forelegs and forcing both of them to crouch; but not before Tom glimpsed a dagger slice the air and felt it cut his cheek.

43

Then the monster disappeared back up into the fog, screaming in frustration as it flew away.

"At last, I have a reason to stop walking," Lady Torka said, her large wings swirling the mist around her as she sprang into the air.

"Run, children!" she said.

In the space her wings had cleared, Tom saw four *jenmien* diving toward her. They had apelike bodies and short, stiff tails, but their heads were like owls' except with noses and mouths instead of beaks. Each of them clutched knives and clubs in their paws.

"Freedom!" Lady Torka honked as she tore into them. Her great wings batted two to either side, and her fangs and spiked fan made the other pair bank sharply to save their own lives.

"I see her point," Räv puffed as she slipped in front of Tom.

They had no sooner taken a few steps when a shaggy-haired woman leaped out and blocked their way. She was as thin as a broom and her arms and legs were like pipe stems. She gave a roar that echoed throughout Chinatown, and Tom heard an answering rumble as if a horde of motorcycle engines had come to life.

Räv slashed at her, forcing her to back up.

"Keep going," Räv said to Tom, waving her free arm. "I can fight better if I don't have to worry about you."

In the pause, the woman had transformed into a *chu*

chien. Her head was human but she now had only a single eye in the center of her face and the tips of her oxlike ears stuck out through her shaggy, spotted hair. Her tail was as long as her leopardlike body. Crouching, she whipped her long tail out so that it curled around Räv's ankle and yanked her from her feet.

"Räv," he said, starting toward her, but she flapped her hand at him.

"Get him out of here, you idiot." And rolling onto her side, she slashed at the tail so that the chu chien let go with a howl.

Tom wanted to stay and help her, but he knew she was right: No one else mattered—certainly neither him nor Räv—as long as the phoenix remained safe.

So he moved on, and had almost reached the store when ten monsters sprang from the fog to surround him.

Tom crouched like a cornered beast. Snarling the words for the wind spell, he shoved his right palm at the nearest attacker and struck the beast with the force of a tornado, sending it spinning away. A blow from his left palm sent another whirling to the side.

Left. Right. Over and over, Tom sent his enemies sprawling.

But the effort left him breathless and tired. As he stumbled on, he felt the ground tremble beneath his feet as a horde of monsters charged toward them. More poured from the rooftops, crawling down the walls in a living tide.

And from the howls and roars and wails coming from all over Chinatown, he knew others must be coming.

From overhead, Tom heard the screeching of jen-mien diving, and he knew his allies were completely surrounded on the ground and above. Mr. Hu's charm could not protect him against so many determined foes. They had finally succeeded in drawing out Vatten's army—but the victory would be Vatten's and not theirs.

"Mama!" the phoenix cried in alarm. All the noise had caused the bird to peer out of the pouch.

Tom glanced down at the frightened, fuzzy face staring up at him. "I'm sorry," he said as he cupped the pouch in his hands. "I wasn't able to keep my promise to you for even an hour."

"Mama hurt," the phoenix said, noticing the cut on Tom's cheek.

The sight of the phoenix drove the monsters into a frenzy. Salivating and roaring, they closed in, shouting: "The bird is Lord Vatten's."

The corners of Tom's mouth drew back to expose his teeth and a growl came from deep in his throat like a file rasping over rough iron.

"Mama, no let them take me," the phoenix peeped shrilly. "Want stay here." His beak clasped Tom's shirt.

"You no let them?" the phoenix asked desperately.

"No," Tom promised, pressing the little bird even closer to him and roaring his defiance. "He's mine!"

Tom tried to gather his last bits of energy so that he could punish as many of their enemies as he could before the end.

As he lifted his hands away from the phoenix, he heard Mr. Hu roar, "I'm coming, Master Thomas." The tiger sprang down beside him, lashing out with his fangs and claws.

A moment later, Tom heard Mistral shouting, "Kamsin! Kamsin!" Her tail, swinging like a club, ripped the fog away from overhead. Hovering, she struck out with her forepaws and fangs at the enemy.

Monkey landed seconds after, his staff sending chu chien sprawling. "Can I crash this party, or do I need an invitation?"

In front of them a manhole cover lifted enough for a yellow snout to poke out. "Sheesh," Sidney said, "I knew you guys would need me out here more than in the store. This way."

The tiger shook his head. "We could be trapped in the sewer."

Lifting the heavy cover on his back, the rat climbed out. "Then I guess we have to get home the hard way." From his fur, he pulled out a newly honed hatchet.

The sight of his friends renewed Tom like a tonic, sending his tiger's blood racing through his weary body so that he'd never felt stronger or more alive. With a roar loud enough to match Mr. Hu's, Tom raised his arm and the wind lashed like a whip, flinging the jen-mien against the walls. The boy was surprised by the unexpected force of his spell. Was this what Mr. Hu had meant about tiger magic coming from the heart?

"Watch it," Räv called. "I'm coming right behind you." He felt her back against him. "Okay, let's go."

But as the monsters pressed forward with their attack, it was all the friends could do to hold their own. The mist disappeared and they could see that the monsters had parted before them, forming a living corridor. Tom wondered if they'd finally given up. But then he saw a tall warrior waiting at the mouth of the alley.

He must have been at least eight feet tall and was so thin in his red-scaled armor that he looked like a snake. His red hair rose up like a lion's mane, and the skin of his face was tinged a sickly pink. He had a sharply pointed nose and protruding tusks that twisted his mouth into an ugly smile. His pupil-less eyes shone like silver-blue mirrors, matching his large rectangular shield.

"Vatten," Räv gasped.

Tom stared. Here was the leader of the monsters who had killed his grandmother.

"How kind of you to deliver the phoenix into my hand, Guardian." Vatten's voice boomed in the suddenly silent street. "Now I can bring order out of chaos."

Panting, Mr. Hu crouched on all fours. Flattening his

ears, he snarled, "Never. Your order is one of death."

"There's another manhole right behind that big wind-bag, Mr. H.," Sidney whispered, then flicked a hindpaw at the hole from which he had emerged. "And that sewer line leads right to him."

"Now you'll see what tiger magic can do, Master Thomas." Mr. Hu reared upward, his muscles swelling beneath his tattered suit, whiskers bristling, and his eyes burning like amber fire. Vatten crouched behind his shield, ready to deflect any magical attack.

Hissing a spell, Mr. Hu pointed his paws not at Vatten, but at the open hole. At first, Tom thought it was the tiger's claws that had grown in length, but then he saw the air shimmer and sizzle, and he realized the claws had become flames shooting into the sewer.

Vatten mocked the tiger from behind his shield. "Your aim is poor, Guardian. Are you that frightened?"

"My aim is excellent," Mr. Hu snarled.

In that instant, the manhole cover behind Vatten flew into the air and fiery claws lanced upward to rake Vatten's legs, exposed below his shield. The scales of his armor bubbled as the claws sliced through them and a strange blue steam rose from his wounded flesh.

Vatten threw up his head in agony and unfurled large, leathery wings like a bat's. With a loud flap and a scream, he lurched into the air.

Mr. Hu's flames stretched after him, but Vatten banked sharply, ricocheting against a wall and then above the roofs and away.

From the street, his followers howled in dismay and those that could fly began to dart after their leader.

"Freedom!" Lady Torka cried from overhead, and there were more cries as dozens of other flying foxes plummeted with her in pursuit; but Vatten's monsters met them and the sky was filled with swirling aerial battles.

"Freedom!" Lord Harnal shouted from farther down the street.

A poster on a wall began to glow and then disappeared in a burst of green light to reveal a dragon charm beneath. The charm swelled in size and brightness until it was large enough that a dragon was able to plunge through and land on the street at the rear of the horde. Skidding on the damp pavement, the dragon used his tail to knock down several monsters and cleared a space for the next dragon to come through the opening.

As more dragons charged into their panicked enemies, a poster at the opposite end of the street burned with a blue glow.

Master Yen had placed his own charms about Chinatown. A warrior, wearing an armor of bronze plates in the shape of maple leaves, clanked onto the pavement. Around his wrists were bracelets in the shape of more maple leaves and in his hand was a spear with a blade also shaped like a leaf.

Identical warriors followed him, one after another, until there were seventy-two of them.

"Hu! Hu!" they called.

And from all about Chinatown, more and more voices were taking up the cry as the Alliance turned the tables on Vatten's monsters.

CHAPTER FOUR

Suan-yü

It has a serpentine body with six eyes and three feet and flies with the aid of four wings. When one sees it, one can be sure trouble will come to one's town.

—Shan Hai Ching

Exhausted, Mr. Hu released his fiery claws and collapsed on the street.

"Mr. Hu!" Tom cried as he dropped to his knees.

The tiger raised a limp paw. "Are you all right, Master Thomas?"

"Yes." Tom puffed.

"And the phoenix?" Mr. Hu asked.

"Scary" was the phoenix's verdict.

"And you, Mistress Räv?"

"Just fine."

The tiger arched a weary eyebrow. "Better than your borrowed clothing, I see."

"Yeah, sorry." She hunched her shoulders, trying to hide the tears in the robe and waiting for a scolding.

The Guardian smiled kindly. "Well, I have another

robe up in the attic; and though it comes from a later dynasty, I trust you'll take better care of that one by not playing with monsters."

"Whatever you say," she promised him fervently.

The dragons and rebels formed a protective band around them. Monkey and Mistral carried the Guardian to his store, which Sidney had left open. With their master's flight, the heart seemed to have left the enemy—and all they could think of was their own escape. There were so many fugitives that the Alliance could not capture them all, but they were trying.

Within the store, Tom and Räv tended the tiger, though he insisted that all he really needed was some rest. Even the phoenix huddled in his box. It frightened Tom to see the lively bird grow so quiet, and he took the bird upon his lap.

Tom tried to think of something to comfort the chick. "My grandma used to take care of you and me before Mr. Hu took over, did you know that?" He petted the bird delicately with a fingertip.

"Grandma?" the phoenix asked curiously.

"That'd make her your great-grandma." Tom couldn't help smiling. "She'd tell you that it's not your fault if you're special. And if you want to stay here, that's your right."

Of course, the phoenix wanted to look at his favorite book next, but unfortunately there was no picture of a great-grandmother in it. Still, seeing the pictures of the family cheered the little bird. And when, on the twentieth reading, Tom tried to skip a page, the phoenix looked up from his lap and laughed. "Mama make mistake."

"Yeah, Mama made a mistake," Tom said. "I don't know why we have to read this to you anymore. You've got it memorized."

"Quit being so crabby, Mama." Räv held up her hands so she could view the two of them through the frame formed by her fingers. "You know, I think he's getting to look like you too."

"Really?" Tom asked slyly. "I think his beak looks more like his papa's."

"Papa, Papa!" the phoenix chimed, and raised his head to look at Räv.

"I am not, and never will be, anyone's father."

"A parent then," Tom said.

"Forget it." She hunched her shoulders. "I'd be rotten at it." But the bird seemed to have gotten beneath her mask of toughness, as usual.

Tom stroked the back of the phoenix. The bird was definitely larger and felt bonier, as if he were growing extremely fast. "You've been helping with the phoenix just fine."

"Don't get the wrong idea," she said. "I've got to do something to keep from getting bored." To prove her point, she tilted her chair back and set her feet sullenly upon an antique table.

54

When Tom got to the page about the grandfather, the phoenix pointed his beak at the resting Mr. Hu. "Grandpa."

Mr. Hu's eyes shot open. "What? I never . . ." he spluttered.

"If I'm stuck being the father, then you can be the grandfather," Räv said.

"You should be honored, Hu, old boy," Monkey drawled lazily. "Since the phoenix is King of the Birds, that makes you royalty."

"Uncle," the phoenix said.

"No, and thank your lucky stars." Monkey grinned.

Mr. Hu returned the favor. "It's your turn to be honored. Welcome to the royal bird family."

Pleased, the phoenix looked at Mistral next. "Auntie."

Mistral was rebandaging a cut on her leg. "Well, we both have wings, so I guess that does make us kin, but I refuse to be related to this furbag ape."

"Uncle Furbag," the phoenix said with satisfaction.

"Now hold on," Monkey said indignantly, but Sidney pushed past him. "Hey, kiddo, don't forget Uncle Sidney."

"No Uncle. You Doggy," the phoenix said, pointing a wing at the family's pet in the picture book.

"You mean Ratty." Monkey chuckled.

Sidney patted his chest. "No, I'm an uncle too."

But the bird picked up a pen in his beak and, with a twist of his head, threw it a foot away. "Fetch, Doggy."

With great persistence Sidney tried to correct the

phoenix, and with equal stubbornness the chick insisted he was a pet and should fetch the "stick."

Tom and the others could not stop laughing. It was the first light moment in a long time and everyone—except poor Sidney—enjoyed it as if they truly were a family, albeit an odd one.

It was Lady Torka who brought the good news, tapping at the door with one paw to be let in. There was blood on her fur, even redder than her hair, and her wings were no longer snow white, but she smiled wearily. "We've smashed Vatten's army. The ones we haven't captured are streaming away from the city. Master Yen will be lifting his spell on the humans soon."

"I safe?" the phoenix asked.

"Yes, Your Highness," the Lady Torka said with a deep bow.

As the others cheered, the rat's fur began to spread out with a humming sound and he flew up into the air and began to whirl around.

"Yippee," Sidney cried. The ecstatic rat rummaged around in his fur. "Now, where did I put those party hats?"

Mr. Hu used his free paw to snag the rat's tail. "You fool rat, this is no time to celebrate." He looked at Lady Torka. "What news of Vatten? Have you caught him?"

"No," Lady Torka said, waving her wings in dismissal, "but it's only a matter of time."

Sidney flew in a slow circle over the Guardian's head, his tail still caught in the tiger's grip. "Yeah, see? So don't be a killjoy, Mr. H."

Räv was quick to side with her hero. "Mr. Hu's right. Vatten's a master shape-shifter, and he could still cause a lot of trouble."

Lady Torka hid her mouth politely behind a wingtip but they could hear her chuckling. "How? Without an army, he can't do anything."

Mr. Hu shook his head. "He could destroy the Imperfect Mountain."

From the Lore, Tom knew it was one of the pillars of Heaven. When Kung Kung, Vatten's master, had been defeated in that first great war, his last act was to strike his head against the mountain. And when it began to crumble, it could no longer support the sky, and the heavens themselves began to crack. The Empress Nü Kua had repaired the sky, but ever since, people had called the pillar the Imperfect Mountain.

Mr. Hu stared at the floor for a long time, lost in thought, twitching his tail. "Vatten's pride is nearly as strong as his thirst for vengeance. He'll want to succeed where his master failed and destroy the mountain, the sky, and the world."

"If he's alive, he won't escape us," Lady Torka declared confidently.

Mr. Hu's whiskers twitched skeptically. "I hope so," he said, "for all our sakes."

Over the next week, letters materialized from all around the world, bringing news of victories everywhere. Vatten's monsters were either dead, captured, or fleeing; but the Guardian took no pleasure because there was still no word about Vatten's fate—and yet the Alliance was withdrawing forces from the hunt.

And he was positively outraged when the only response to all his worried letters he sent out was an invitation to a victory celebration at Master Yen's Sky Palace.

"Fools, it's still premature," the tiger grumbled, crumpling up the card.

"Can you blame them? It has been such a long, hard struggle that they want to think this nightmare is finally over," Mistral said. "When the desire is strong enough, people will ignore facts and believe what they want to."

"All the leaders of the Alliance will be there," Räv pointed out.

"Hmm, yes." Mr. Hu nodded. "We'll go, not to celebrate, but to talk some sense into them. They must unite again to catch Vatten. But in the meantime, I'm sure we can get you an escort if you want to visit your home," he added.

"There'll be time for that later," the girl said hastily.

"They're in San Francisco, after all, and they know where I am."

Mr. Hu gazed at her thoughtfully. "In all this time, you've never called your family. Don't you want to do that now?"

"They must still be busy with the war." Räv straightened her new robe. True to his word, the Guardian had gone up to the attic and brought down a beautiful purple one embroidered with flowers.

Even though he believed their mission was urgent, Mr. Hu still insisted that they all present their best appearance. That meant Tom had to iron the Guardian's suit, which he did conscientiously, if not well, and Mistral polished her scales with some of Sidney's best car polish, trying to hide her scars, the souvenirs of her many battles. Tom also bathed the phoenix and brushed his feathers to a fine sheen. Monkey prepared in his own way by hunting around the store until he had found an old clothespin.

The magical gate to Master Yen's palace opened promptly on the date on the invitation and was predictably garish, with ruby posts and a golden sign that flashed:

"WELCOME, GREAT GUARDIAN!"

Mr. Hu shaded his eyes against the glare with one paw, while, with another, he slipped the handkerchief from his pocket and covered his nostrils as cloying perfume flooded into the room. "Egad! Why can't Master Yen's taste equal his magic?"

Sidney ran up to the gate to admire it. "Oh, I don't know, Mr. H. If you had one of these babies for your store, you might pull in some customers."

Mr. Hu's indignant voice was muffled by his handkerchief. "I am running an antique store, not a casino."

Wearing a blue antique robe Mr. Hu had given him, Tom followed the Guardian obediently through the gate. There was a moment when he felt himself being pushed and pulled by the wind—like invisible hands tugging him this way and that—and then he was on the threshold.

He halted when he saw only thin air beyond. Below him were mountains like half-melted lumps of candy and rivers like dark blue ribbons and a lake or sea that shone red in the setting sun.

"Don't dawdle, Master Thomas. We must warn the other leaders," Mr. Hu said, gesturing impatiently with his paw. Tom thought the Guardian was standing in midair, but then he realized the tiger was actually on a cloud—no, not a cloud, but a cable of mist. Tom continued to hesitate on the threshold.

"It's really quite safe," Mr. Hu assured him brusquely and patted the cable with a hind paw, giving off a faint whiff of incense. "The Sky Palace is made entirely of a mist that is light enough to ride the wind currents and yet is stronger than any steel." He held out his forepaw. "Trust me. With my blood in you, you will have my balance."

If the tiger had not constantly risked his life to save Tom, the boy would never have stepped through the gate. He stretched out his hand, but it shook noticeably.

Inside the pouch, the phoenix sensed the tension in his mother's body and began to chirp anxiously. "You is scared, Mama?"

"Set an example for my um . . . grandson," Mr. Hu coaxed with a smile.

Tom let himself be pulled out onto the cable and was alarmed to feel how it swayed, but the motion was only slight. And it was solid enough, if a bit spongy beneath his feet, as well as dry for good footing; and since it was about six inches wide, it was broad enough to walk on but narrow enough to seem as though he were walking on thin air. Though he would rather have taken the time to get used to the strange sensation, Tom allowed Mr. Hu to guide him farther along the cable to make room for the others.

He was surprised to find that Mr. Hu's prediction was right and that his body knew exactly how and where to move. However, he wished he'd brought a clothespin like Monkey had, as each step released a whiff of perfume, each slightly different. He felt as if he had put his face into a bowl of potpourri.

Mistral was not as impressed by the aerial view, being used to flying high in the sky. Räv did her best to imitate the dragon's casual attitude, but stayed close to her for safety. The ever-curious Sidney scampered along, feeling the cable, perhaps to see if it had any value for bartering.

"Hurry up, Doggy," the phoenix called, peering from his pouch.

"For the umpteenth time, it's *Uncle Sidney*," the rat said.

Monkey was last, and he ambled through, his cap pulled down over his head and the clothespin over his nostrils.

As he walked along, Tom noticed that the palace's cables, tinted pink in the sunset, extended above and below him, weaving into a misty lace and forming a giant, multilevel globe. Though the cables kept swaying ever so slightly, they stayed part of the intricate design. It seemed like a colossal game of cat's cradle, but the farther in they went, the more complex the lace became. He could almost, but not quite, make out the strokes of Chinese letters and words, and even the ancient serpentine runes of the dragons, in the pattern of the lace. Like a feather, the meaning tickled his mind.

Using his beak, the phoenix attempted to snatch a wisp that floated by. "Don't," Tom ordered. "We don't know what it really is."

"But I is hungry," the phoenix complained.

"You'll get to eat soon," Tom assured him.

Within the misty lace, the air was still and heavy with the scent of flowers, but outside it, clouds quickly scudded by, as if strong winds drove them above the darkening world. The invitation had said the palace would be above China, but all they could see was uncivilized wilderness below.

The path led them to a center point, where the cables had been wound so tightly that they formed a titanic ball of yarn. A silvery, iridescent light radiated from this central orb, so that from a distance, it resembled a huge pearl.

Tom caught faint snatches of music floating through the intricate web; now here, now there. Cascading notes played on some unknown instrument resonated with a strange pleasantness deep inside Tom, as though his heart heard it better than his ears.

The mysterious, lovely song drew them all eagerly; and as one, they hurried forward until they reached a giant portal, glittering as though stars had settled on it to rest before flying off into the night sky. Large, coiled serpents, with double pairs of wings like a dragonfly's, stood guard on either side of the portal. Each serpent had three paws, one of which held a small wicker shield, while the other two paws held short cutlasses. As the sentries slithered to attention, Tom heard the telltale creaking of their joints, and he realized they must be more of Master Yen's robotic creatures.

"*Suan-yü*," Mr. Hu hissed. "Why re-create such ill-omened creatures? The living originals made nothing but trouble." He tucked his handkerchief back into his coat pocket and glanced at the ape. "You'd better take off that clothespin. You'll insult our host."

"All right." Monkey sighed as he reluctantly removed it and wrinkled his nose. "But I don't have to like it."

"Hungry, Mama," the phoenix peeped from the pouch.

Tom put a reassuring hand on him. "I promise I'll feed you soon."

They entered a corridor that appeared to curl toward the heart of the palace, passing rooms filled with tapestries and artwork. Inside the rooms, books, strange weapons, and magical apparatuses were piled everywhere, and many of the chairs and benches seemed designed for odd-shaped bodies.

They could hear the music clearly now, as well as laughter and conversation. Sidney rubbed his paws together gleefully. "Oh, boy!" he said. "Let me at 'em. Happy voices mean spending customers."

Mr. Hu bent over and grabbed the rat by the scruff of his neck. "Listen, you fool rat. You are *not*, under any circumstances, to bother any of the guests with commemorative snow globes. Or else our host is likely to change you into a toad. And I won't lift a claw to defend you."

"Hu," Mistral said as she strolled along, "Master Yen's got much more imagination than that. He'll turn Sidney into something a lot more interesting than a toad."

"Heh, heh. You're a real pair of kidders." Sidney laughed nervously as he glanced between the tiger and the dragon, but they only stared at him, as stern and grim as statues. When he realized they were perfectly serious, he gulped. "He wouldn't really pick on a fellow for trying to make a living, would he?"

"It's how he would handle any pest," Mr. Hu growled.

"Those that he lets live, that is," Mistral added.

Sidney wrung his paws. "Yeah, but . . . I mean . . . Gee, a guy's got to get by, doesn't he? I mean, I got five dozen glossy photos of the phoenix and you, Mr. H."

"What?" the tiger burst out indignantly. "How dare you!"

Selling was instinctual to the rat, so Tom could see trouble ahead. "Well, what if Sidney promised to sell only to the servants and warriors?" he suggested.

Sidney gave a little hop. "Yeah, that's a great idea. They'll probably buy more because they'll be bored. Quantity can be better than quality."

Mr. Hu shut his eyes with long-suffering patience. "Oh, very well. If you must. But no photos."

"Gotcha, Mr. H. No autographed pix," the relieved rat agreed, giving his own interpretation to things. And then he nudged the boy. "You know, Tom, if this apprenticeship doesn't work with Mr. H., you come see me."

CHAPTER FIVE

Master Yen
*There once was a wizard who created robots so lifelike that people
thought they were alive. He used leather, wood, gum, lacquer, and
the magical colors of white, black, red, and blue.*

Ch'ih Yu
*When a mountain split open in an earthquake, he was the first to take
the ore he found and make metal weapons. His head was of bronze
and his brow of iron and he dined on stone pebbles. He was fond of
jokes and dancing and created a head-butting dance that people
performed into the time of the Han dynasty. He has seventy-two brothers.*

The Dark Lady
*Her head was human but she had a bird's body. She taught the
legendary Yellow Emperor how to best his enemies and helped him
create the Chinese empire.*

K'ua Fu
*Yellow snakes lived upon the sides of his heads and on his hands.
He was so strong and fast he could catch the sun's shadow.*
—Tradition

The sentries must have alerted their master somehow, because Master Yen was waiting before a pair of huge doors at the end of the corridor. He was wearing an orange robe decorated flamboyantly with violet feathers on the cuffs and hem, almost as garish as his gate signs.

"Welcome, Guardian!" he said, bowing to Mr. Hu. "We have all been waiting for you and His Highness," he said, nodding at the phoenix, who was peering out of the pouch.

The suan-yü opened the doors, revealing a huge, spherical chamber that pulsed with a soft, silvery light. In place of a solid floor, many small platforms were suspended in the air all around them, hanging from ribbons of mist as fine as spider thread—not that many at the gathering needed them, for they hovered in the air, flitting about like butterflies.

There did not seem to be an up or down in the chamber either. Some merrymakers were standing upright while others were sideways or even upside down, chatting and laughing, unconcerned with the laws of gravity.

The folk gathered went all the way back to the time of the world's creation. And although they had defeated Kung Kung and had saved the world several times over, their exploits had taken place so long ago, even China had forgotten them. There were no statues of them in any of the stores and temples of Chinatown—there were only tributes to the most recent heroes—thus, Tom hadn't recognized any of them when they had first come to forge the Alliance at Mr. Hu's store.

Since then, he'd read about many of the celebrants in brittle scrolls so dusty that they made him cough; but it was awe-inspiring to see them now in the flesh—a lesson in living history.

Some were in gorgeous robes of costly silk and wearing jewelry by the ton. Others wore modern clothes that could have come out of some fashion magazine. A large number were human in appearance, but many were shaped like strange animals and several had no form at all but floated like patches of shining mist.

Räv murmured, "It's like a painting." She could smile with reckless courage when she was battling monsters, but the glittering spectacle seemed to intimidate her, and she wound her robe more tightly around herself as though it offered some kind of magic protection.

What intimidated the girl only encouraged the enterprising rat, who was eagerly looking about. "Yeah, where there's this much jewelry, there's always a need for polish."

"Have a care," Mistral reminded the rat.

Sidney's fur began to vibrate, so that he looked like a small yellow shrub shaking in the wind. "I got you. I was going to find their butlers and maids. They got to be somewhere in this joint."

"Our celebration can truly begin now that you are

here." Beckoning for them to follow, Master Yen raised his arms, and the feathers on the cuffs and hem of his robe began to flutter, drawing him up into the air.

"It will be just like swimming, Master Thomas," Mr. Hu said, and with an encouraging smile at his apprentice, he leaped lithely into the chamber.

Mistral gave Tom a gentle nudge. "Whoops, how clumsy of me," she said as the boy stumbled into the chamber, where he floundered wildly for a moment until the Guardian snagged him by the sleeve.

"I see we must work on your entrances as well," said the tiger.

Safe in his master's grip, Tom stopped struggling and found that, through some magical spell, the air supported him—as if he were swimming in water.

A second later, Räv tumbled head over heels toward them and would have sailed past if Tom, who remembered she could not swim, had not caught her with his free hand.

"I'll get you later," she muttered over her shoulder at the dragon.

Mistral sprang upward, her paws folded in the picture of innocence. "Better to be thought clumsy than afraid," she murmured as she drifted by.

The wizard raised his hand, and pipes shrilled triumphantly before the crash of cymbals and huge drums drowned them out. As vast as the chamber was, Tom and his friends felt as if they were in the middle of a thunder cloud.

The deafening noise so startled the little bird that he dove back into his pouch. "It's all right," Tom said, though he knew his reassurances were lost in the music.

With a worried glance at the phoenix, Mr. Hu roared to their host: "Less noise, if you please. You're scaring the guest of honor."

Master Yen cupped a hand behind his ear and shook his head to indicate he hadn't heard; the frustrated tiger had to let go of his apprentice and pantomime with increasingly violent gestures until the wizard finally understood and signaled to his musicians to stop the march.

"A thousand apologies." Master Yen bowed.

Mr. Hu gave a roaring cough. "How can we celebrate while Vatten is still loose?" he demanded.

Ch'ih Yu dropped toward them. He wore armor with leaf-shaped scales when he went into battle, but tonight he was in a robe decorated with maple leaves. His bronze head had been burnished until it shone.

His metallic lips turned up with a creak as he spoke. "We've all read your letters. All that worrying is going to turn your fur gray, Guardian."

The Dark Lady fluttered upward. When Tom had first met her at the conference, he thought her dark blue-and-black clothing was like a theatrical costume matching her skin, but when he had gotten closer, he saw that her headdress was a helmet and the feathers on it and her blouse and trousers were actually cunningly wrought scales of armor. "Three cheers for the Guardian!" she called.

Ch'ih Yu punched a fist at the air and spun like a top, shouting in a resounding voice, "Yes, three cheers for the Guardian!"

Hand and paw, hoof and tentacle were raised in salute, and voices rose in a chorus of shouts, roars, and howls of greeting. The phoenix hid inside his pouch. With each cheer, the sound grew louder. Mr. Hu fidgeted uncomfortably; Tom was sure that if the tiger had been in his human form, he would have been blushing.

Tom could feel the phoenix shivering. Letting go of Räv, who was able to float on her own, he cupped his hand over his shirt protectively. He felt the little bird calm down and press back trustingly.

Even while the last hurrah was echoing from the walls, Mr. Hu put up his paws. The tiger had never been a patient creature. "I didn't come to celebrate," he roared over the noise. "I came to warn you."

The tattooed warrior K'ua Fu floated down to them. At their initial meeting, everyone had been very careful not to excite him, though Tom could not understand why. His face was battered and scarred from many battles, but so were many other of the veteran warriors; and the tattoos of yellow snakes around his ears and on the back of his hands were no worse than Tom had seen on people in Market Street.

"All in good time, all in good time," K'ua Fu said, "but first we want to see the phoenix again."

The others seemed just as determined to ignore the Guardian's worries.

"Yes," the Dark Lady said, "we want to see the darling little creature. I haven't seen him since we formed the Alliance."

The crowd had formed a ring around them by now and they all clamored to see the phoenix.

"Better do what they want," Mistral counseled, "or we'll never be able to warn them."

With a sigh, Mr. Hu looked over his shoulder. "Master Thomas?"

"I'm not sure if he wants to come out," Tom said, looking around at the intimidating throng. "He's awfully scared." He spoke soothingly to the phoenix. "It's okay. No one's going to harm you."

He felt the little bird wrap its claws delicately around his fingers and hold on tightly as he drew it out. There were admiring murmurs as Tom held the phoenix up in both palms.

"Welcome, Lord of all the Birds." The Dark Lady bowed.

Kings and queens, warriors and wizards and sorceresses

all dipped their heads respectfully. The silence seemed to unnerve the phoenix even more than the cheering had. He quivered upon Tom's hand, all his feathers bristling, then skittered frantically up the boy's arm and hopped back into his pouch.

As everyone else laughed, K'ua Fu rubbed his temple and Tom would have sworn that the tattooed snake coiled around his ear wriggled. "He's growing so fast. Soon we'll have peace around the world so there won't be any need for an old fighter like me."

"I think we'll still want your services, friend," Mr. Hu said. "His birth was premature. He's supposed to be born only *after* the world is at peace."

"And there is the irony, isn't it?" The Dark Lady's shrug sent her drifting through the air. "He has the ability to stop all violence, but he shouldn't need to use it because everyone should be at peace before his birth."

"You've misinterpreted what happened in my kingdom, Guardian, but I forgive you for being overly sensitive," the Dragon King countered huffily from above. Wriggling behind him was the dragon warrior Tench, who had trapped Mistral's friend Ring Neck. "We were simply examining the egg to make sure it was intact after all its travels," he said, not the least bit apologetic over the dragons' theft of the egg to hatch it and use the phoenix's power against their enemies.

Mistral glowered. "That's not what you said to me."

The king looked down his long snout as he leisurely descended toward them. "Then you misunderstood me as well." His words sounded like a warning.

Smooth as silk, Master Yen glided between them. "You've made that quite clear, Your Majesty. And we accept your word."

Mistral reared her head up, ready to object, when Mr. Hu stopped her. "Don't fracture the Alliance now. We need diplomacy, not truth."

"Diplomacy be hanged," Mistral spat out.

The Dragon King kept his voice pleasant enough, but his eyes narrowed menacingly. "What has the truth won you except exile—twice?"

For once, it was the ape who was the soul of caution. Monkey had slipped into the chamber while all eyes were on the phoenix and threw himself upon Mistral before she could charge at the king.

Anxiously, Master Yen swam about. "Please remember that you are both guests, and that my palace is neutral territory."

"It looks as if you need the phoenix's power at this moment." The Dragon King laughed.

"He hasn't matured enough yet," Mr. Hu said, "and until he does, we must make sure that Vatten—"

"Let's not be tedious, Guardian," the Dark Lady warned.

The little bird, seeing how upset the tiger was becoming,

overcame his shyness enough to say, "You be good. Listen to Grandpa. Please."

"Grandpa?" K'ua Fu laughed.

The phoenix glared at the warrior angrily. "He is Grandpa."

"As Your Highness requests," K'ua Fu said with an acknowledging bow.

Mr. Hu's growl boomed through the chamber. "Half of us should join the hunt for Vatten. The other half should go to the Imperfect Mountain to guard it against his vengeance. Open a gate there now."

Master Yen fluttered a hand. "Oh my, how you flatter me. But even a wizard as mighty as I cannot open a gate to the Imperfect Mountain. The lines of ch'i there are so powerful they interfere with the spells."

"Then we fly there," Mr. Hu argued.

"Why bother? Didn't you carve Vatten up like a haunch of beef?" K'ua Fu asked. "How far can he and his followers run? The younger lords and ladies will track them down in whatever hole they're hiding in."

Tom knew by now that the "younger lords and ladies" were the more familiar Chinese heroes and spirits, who appeared as statues on the Chinatown altars and in the books of myths. Though they might be a thousand years old, they would seem like children to these ancient warriors.

Mr. Hu stiffened. "I think you underestimate Vatten.

We should be using every resource. As soon as he's healed, he'll be heading to the Imperfect Mountain."

"Tut, tut, I think you underestimate your martial prowess." The Dark Lady raised a hand to stop Mr. Hu from arguing further. "Don't you think we considered Vatten's thirst for vengeance? We've already dispatched a guard to the mountain, but we'll catch him long before he can reach it."

"How large a force did you send?" Mr. Hu demanded.

K'ua Fu gave the tiger a patronizing smile. "More than enough. Don't spoil our fun, Guardian, by being such a worrywart."

Räv immediately sprang to Mr. Hu's defense. "Are you calling the Guardian a liar?"

There was a fluttering at the sides of K'ua Fu's head, and again Tom could have sworn the tattoos had come to life. "I trust you're not calling me one?" he asked dangerously.

"No, of course she isn't," Master Yen assured K'ua Fu. Under his breath, he muttered, "Now, now, let's not get K'ua Fu upset by arguing, shall we?"

At his signal, the orchestra began playing a gentle melody on jade chimes. Rectangular slabs, some as huge as Mr. Hu and others as small as the phoenix, hung from golden frames. With their paws and tail holding wool-covered mallets, robotic suan-yü tapped the precious jade to produce the strange, enchanting notes. The crowd began to glide about the chamber, away from the fuming tiger.

Mr. Hu roared in frustration, "Fools! You're hiding your heads in the sand!"

All Master Yen did was signal the orchestra to play louder.

CHAPTER SIX

The K'uei

*He looks like an ox with only one hind leg. His body is dark green
and glistens and his bellows sound like thunder. Wind and rain
come wherever he passes.*

—Shan Hai Ching

Mr. Hu hovered, whipping his tail in exasperation.
And the gesture made him slowly spin, like a lazy
top.

Räv flailed at the air as she tried to reach the Guardian;
it was more her momentum than her skill that carried her
over to him. "My fellow rebels will believe you," she
announced proudly. "They sent me to you because they
respect you so much."

Tom remembered the doubts that Lord Harnal had
expressed when the phoenix was missing. "Are you sure
about this?" he asked cautiously.

Räv was still feeling especially pleased that she could
help the Guardian. "Mr. Hu drove Vatten away himself.
Why wouldn't they believe him?"

"Lead me to them," the worried tiger growled.

Monkey grunted as he kept an eye on Mistral. "I'll take the lizard to a quiet spot where no one will notice us."

Tom glanced behind him. "Where's Sidney?"

"He's already slipped away to peddle his junk." Monkey shrugged.

"I saw Lady Torka over on that platform." Räv made a valiant attempt to move forward but only managed to flounder. Tom stretched out his hand toward her. Even as she struggled to right herself, Räv refused to take it. "I don't want to be towed along like some blimp. People will laugh."

The phoenix waved his wings from the pouch. "Come on, Papa. We is family."

"Just tell me where to go and I'll take you," Tom coaxed. "And in the meantime, you'll get the hang of it." He added softly, "Trust me like I trust you."

"I'm only doing this for Mr. Hu," she grumbled, and lowering her eyes, she took his hand.

Tom headed in the direction Räv indicated. At first he had to pull her, but she soon began to copy his swimming motions.

Adorned with jewelry and robes as lavish as those of anyone else in the chamber, Lady Torka and Lord Harnal sat at a table on a platform. With them were a trio of *k'uei*, hornless oxen, each of whom balanced on a single hind leg. They wore gemmed robes with gold thread, but their limbs revealed a slick, dark-green hide glistening with a pearly sheen.

"I'll take it from here," Räv said when they were only a few yards away. Once Tom had released her, she paddled the rest of the way with as much dignity as she could muster under the circumstances.

Lady Torka lifted her wings partway in salute. "I see you've finally arrived, Ambassador. Now our celebration can truly begin."

Räv bowed first to the winged fox and then to the quilled pig, greeting them by name. Then she dipped her head to the largest of the oxen. "Lord Trumma, I know you will heed the Guardian's warning, because of all the people here, you alone know how dangerous Vatten is. You first sent me to Mr. Hu so he could tell everyone about Vatten's plans."

The phoenix added urgently, "You listen to Grandpa."

"What can we do but obey?" Lady Torka laughed.

"You talk, Grandpa," the phoenix directed Mr. Hu. The little chick seemed to enjoy being the center of attention at the party, and in fact was beginning to get quite bossy.

Mr. Hu and Räv did their best to convince the rebel leaders; but as Tom expected, they seemed as satisfied as their allies that the world was safe from Vatten. They grew increasingly impatient and their replies became short and curt. Even when the phoenix tried to command them to go, they politely refused.

"When you're full grown, Your Highness," Lord Trumma said, "we won't have any choice but to obey. But right now we do."

Räv floated above them, stunned, and then in desperation she held out her hands in appeal. "Please, Lady and Lords. If you value our friendship, listen to me."

Lady Torka pretended to be busy fluffing her wings. "But that's what we're doing. You're the one not listening to us. Everything is fine."

"Now paddle somewhere else, girl," Lord Harnal said, waving his trotter. "Enjoy the evening. We'll catch Vatten long before he can get to that mountain."

"How?" Räv persisted. "We've heard that the rebels are pulling forces from the hunt and returning them home."

Lord Trumma fluttered his scarf to indicate the heroes and dragons around the chamber. "Ask our allies why they are doing the same thing."

Mr. Hu's chin sank to his chest. "I see," he said softly. "So that's the real reason none of you will listen to me. It didn't take long for old fears to resurrect themselves and crumble the Alliance. You think Vatten is less of a threat now than your former allies."

"We've hated one another almost as long as we've hated Vatten. He's no danger to us now, but *they* still are."

Lord Harnal's quills rattled as he jerked his head at the heroes and dragons. "They've been our mortal enemies all these centuries. They've killed countless of our kin. Let's say we follow your advice and keep all our forces in pursuit of Vatten, but *they* only pretend to? Who's going to defend our homes and families from them while our armies are off chasing a wounded beggar?"

"No doubt the dragons and others are giving in to the same suspicions." Mr. Hu shook his head. "But you're wrong to dismiss Vatten as harmless. The Alliance must hold together for a little while longer. Then you can go back to your ancient feuds."

Lord Harnal frowned. "We've just escaped one master. Why should we listen to the reckless schemes of a new one like you? You Guardians have never had our interests at heart either."

Mr. Hu stiffened. "You used me to put together the Alliance so you could rid yourself of your former leader. And now that you think he's gone, you're discarding me as well." He squared his shoulders. "Very well. Bring your forces home, but at least strengthen the guard at the Imperfect Mountain."

"We'll take it under consideration." Lady Torka shrugged.

"Meaning you won't do anything." Räv spread her arms as she pleaded, and the motion made her drift backward. "You've got to listen to the Guardian. If he says you need to reinforce the Imperfect Mountain, then you have to believe him."

The argument had exhausted Lord Harnal's patience, and he snorted in disgust. "Pah! Who are you to tell us what to do? You've no family, no name. We never should have let a street urchin like you become familiar with us. It's gone to your head. We only came to you because we were so desperate."

Lady Torka flapped a wing against him so that he drifted upward from his seat. "Lord Harnal, you needn't be so rude."

Lord Harnal rubbed his quills. "I guess I got carried away, girl—"

"Ambassador," Lord Trumma corrected him.

"You be nice to Papa," the phoenix scolded the rebels.

Lord Trumma's eyes widened and then his shoulders shook as he began to giggle. Rising on his hind leg, he bowed elaborately to the phoenix. "I beg your pardon, Your Highness. We had no idea she was your . . . papa." He turned and tittered to Lord Harnal. "Have more respect for royalty, Harnal."

Lord Harnal slapped his trotters against his sides and began to guffaw. "That's why she's got such a swelled head. She's the phoenix's papa." He laughed so hard that his quills rattled like a hundred knitting needles.

The phoenix yelled shrilly at the pig and oxen: "No laugh at Papa."

It was all Tom could do to keep the phoenix from climbing out of his pouch to protect his father. Remembering how much mischief the little bird's beak had caused in Chinatown, he frantically reminded the chick, "No hurt."

Though Räv seemed close to tears, she was capable of defending her own honor. She raised her head and for a moment her silver hair looked like a helmet. "I'd rather be related to him than to pompous fools like you."

Lord Harnal lunged forward angrily and Lady Torka spread a snow-white wing like a feathered wall to block him. "I think everyone has said enough for tonight," she asserted. "Perhaps you'd best go."

Mr. Hu put a paw on the girl's shoulder. "Come, Ambassador. It's no use. I can see their minds are set on many things."

"Yes, come, Papa," cooed the phoenix from his pouch.

Stiff with anger, her lips pressed together, Räv let herself be pulled away by the tiger.

"It's always the same. People treat you nice only as long as they need you," she said bitterly. "Why don't I ever learn? Stupid, stupid, stupid. And now you know the truth."

"So you really don't have a family?" Tom asked.

She laughed bleakly. "I grew up alone, just like they said."

"Don't you have anybody?" Tom asked.

She shook her head.

Mr. Hu said gently, "True nobility doesn't come at birth; it has to be earned."

"Yeah?" Räv smirked doubtfully.

The Guardian nodded. "The war against Vatten isn't over yet. You'll have ample opportunity to demonstrate your inner character."

"We is family now," the phoenix declared.

The girl's shoulders hunched defensively. "I'll just screw that up like I do everything else."

"Never," the phoenix swore earnestly as he waved a wing back and forth between them. "Me you is together always."

The girl gave a crooked grin as she chucked the little bird under his beak. "Because you're either too stupid or too lazy to get rid of me."

"No, no, I love you," the phoenix chirped, rubbing his beak along Räv's fingers.

"He always means what he says," Mr. Hu said, gazing at her. "Why are you afraid of being loved? Aren't you worthy of it?"

The girl stared at the Guardian. "Am I?"

"Of course," Mr. Hu said, giving her shoulder a

squeeze. "You'll always have a place with us."

The girl wiped at her eyes clumsily. "Until you don't need me anymore. And then I'll be back on the streets."

Mr. Hu flicked the silk handkerchief from his coat pocket and held it out to her with a flourish. "I thought you had been with me long enough to know that I don't do things that way."

She smiled at him gratefully. She took the handkerchief and dabbed at her eyes with one hand while her other brushed across the fine fuzz of the phoenix's head. "I know what Junior's saying now, but let's see what he says when he grows up."

They tried to convince others at the gathering but met the same indifference everywhere. When they tried to speak to Ch'ih Yu and the Dark Lady again, they were more intent on their eating contest than on listening to the Guardian. Ch'ih Yu was eating from a special tray filled with pebbles of all kinds, from quartz to granite. The bronze-headed warrior crushed them between his iron teeth while the Dark Lady revealed teeth filed to triangular points as she consumed pebbles from another bowl. Judging by Ch'ih Yu's glower and the Dark Lady's smile, he was losing.

The phoenix watched their moving jaws and piped up, "Hungry, Mama. Feed now!"

The last thing Tom wanted was for the bird to rampage

through the palace seeking a meal as he had in Chinatown.

The suan-yü wriggled back and forth through the chamber with trays of food and drink. The trays and the dishes on them were of gold and silver and even jade, shaped like giant leaves of various trees. Piled high were candied kumquats and loquats and exotic fruit. There were also pastries of meat or seafood that were baked, steamed, or fried. The other various savories included mounds of spiced sugar loaves shaped as the twelve animals of the Zodiac and rice cakes sweetened with the dew exuded by rare desert plants.

Snagging a cake from a tray, Tom hastily fed some crumbs to the phoenix's snapping beak.

"I suppose we could all use a little refreshment while we decide on our next step. Now where are the others?" Mr. Hu's keen eyes searched the chamber until he saw where Monkey, Mistral, and a very smug-looking Sidney were sitting, then flew toward them.

When they reached the platform, they found Monkey happily stuffing himself with treats from a servant holding three different trays. On one were piled all kinds of desserts, from sweet and heavenly flower cakes to spicy vegetable ones. On another were a bewildering variety of mouthwatering meat pastries. On a third were all manner of tarts made from the fragrant ground seeds of the sea pine, with fillings ranging from rare peaches to pistachio and buffalo cream.

Sidney, his cheek pouches bulging with food, was storing more in his fur as fast as he could snatch it up. Mistral simply sat, her narrowed eyes following every move of the Dragon King.

Tom remembered that Mr. Hu had once told him that only a fool would feud with a dragon, and he was beginning to see why. Keeping Mistral from a fight would be even harder than keeping Räv from one.

"Boy, oh, boy, you should have seen me, Mr. H.," Sidney gloated. "The servants and soldiers were practically mobbing me outside the ballroom. One of the dragons even asked for a can of car polish for the king himself." The rat put up a paw and mimed pasting up a sign. "Just wait until I get home. I'll put up a billboard that says, 'Purveyor to Dragon Royalty.' But you know what sold best?" The rat answered his own question. "Genuine imitation phoenix eggs. I just got a gross from a store and boiled 'em up and then stamped Mr. Hu's mug on it."

"That's outrageous!" the tiger sputtered.

"Ah, don't worry, partner," Sidney said, nudging the Guardian. "I'll give you a cut."

"How can you think of money at a time like this?" Mr. Hu snarled.

"Easy." The rat waved his paw airily—and immediately a jade serving ladle floated out of his fur. He gave them a nervous grin. "Souvenir, you know?"

Mr. Hu ate a meat pastry absently while he thought.

"We'll go to the store first," he finally announced, "and leave the phoenix there. Then Mistral, Monkey, and I," he said, nodding to each in turn, "will go on to the Imperfect Mountain. I'm not going to take their word that they have enough defenders there. I'll see for myself."

"And if they don't?" the ape asked, munching away on one last dumpling.

"Then we stay there until Vatten is killed or captured," Mr. Hu said.

Master Yen danced by, spinning like an upside-down top to the laughter and applause of the crowd, but when he spotted them leaving, he broke off and glided deftly to block their path to the door. "Have you tired of my hospitality so soon, Guardian?"

"I take Vatten seriously even if no one else here does," Mr. Hu said, trying to slip around him.

With a kick, the wizard again slipped in front of the tiger. "I'm afraid I really must insist that you stay for a while."

Mr. Hu straightened. "I am the Guardian of the phoenix, and you cannot tell me when I might or might not go home."

Master Yen gazed at the still-snacking phoenix and dropped his voice. "I didn't want to say this here, but I've heard rumors that there are some people at the party who want His Highness's power for themselves. So perhaps it might be wiser if you stayed with me for a while. My whole staff would be at your disposal, of course."

Mr. Hu narrowed his eyes so they were like amber spear tips. "In other words, I am to be a prisoner."

"Why must you keep twisting my words?" Master Yen said, flapping his arms. "It will be protective custody and only temporary. Let me assure you that I do this only from the love and high regard I have for you."

Mr. Hu looked at him skeptically. "The Alliance agreed to let you be our captor?"

Master Yen squirmed. "Well, um, not exactly. But I'm sure they'll see reason."

"Ah, I see. Whoever catches us gets to keep us." Mr. Hu commented rather loudly to his apprentice, "You will observe, Master Thomas, how quickly temptation has brought out ambition and greed even in the most heroic hearts."

"If we dragons could not resist the temptation, how could you?" Mistral demanded. From Master Yen's startled reaction, the dragon's accusation had struck home. "Yes, the desire for it has already begun working on you, hasn't it?"

"I not want you," the phoenix protested, spraying crumbs all over Master Yen. "We go."

Master Yen brushed off the crumbs. "I want you to consider my palace as your new home, Your Highness. You may malign me all you wish, but the only desire I feel is to protect you." The wizard signed to some snake warriors, who began to undulate toward the chamber's large doorway to block it. "And Guardian, you will find there is no gate back to your store."

CHAPTER SEVEN

Tom looked around the glittering assembly. "There must be someone here who'll help us."

"But who can you trust?" Räv asked.

Mr. Hu surveyed the chamber. "No one, I'm afraid." The tiger struck his head with a paw. "What an idiot I was. I should have left the phoenix back at the store and come here by myself."

"You could open a gate on your own," Monkey suggested.

"But then I would be so exhausted that I couldn't move," Mr. Hu snarled in frustration.

Monkey leaned back, pillowing his head on his paws. "Then we don't have any choice. We'll all have to go to the mountain together."

Sidney gulped as he surveyed the warriorlike creatures floating by the doorway. "You think we can shove those guys out of the way, Mr. H.? They look pretty tough."

Räv folded her arms, gliding upward a few feet. "What you need is some sort of distraction. And I think I know how to provide one."

"Then please do so," Mr. Hu said, tugging his cuffs over his wrists. "We've dallied here long enough."

She was delighted that the tiger had turned to her for help. "Watch brains put brawn into action."

After she had whispered her plan into the tiger's ear, he smiled. "Turn their strength against them!"

"I'll need your help, Monkey." Bouncing upward, the girl caught hold of Monkey's robe and explained her scheme to him softly. As he listened, a grin spread from ear to ear.

"Remind me not to get on your bad side," Monkey said, nodding eagerly.

"This is nothing," Räv said nonchalantly.

"Don't take any big risks," Mr. Hu warned her.

"My whole life has been one big risk," she declared, although she looked pleased with his concern. With a kick, she dove dramatically from the platform—and proceeded to flounder in the air.

"Is this going to take long?" Mistral chuckled.

Cheeks reddening, she remembered what Tom had shown her and began to paddle awkwardly. "I'm going as fast as I can."

"Stay in your pouch," Tom said to the phoenix. He

leaped after her. "Come on."

"I'm tired of looking like a blimp," Räv said, slapping his hand away.

"Then we'll make it seem like you're helping me, okay?" Tom said in a low voice. He drifted slightly behind her and held on to one arm so it looked as if she were pulling him over to the rebel leaders, when in fact he was pushing her.

"I hope you haven't come to lecture us again," Lord Harnal said. His snout was deeply buried in a whole tray of desserts, custard dripping from his jowls.

Räv bowed her head. "No, I've learned my lesson, and I'm sorry to bother you. But it's just that . . . well, I couldn't let the insult to you pass. Whatever you may think of me, I am a rebel. What touches your honor touches mine."

"I thought your days of spying were over," Lady Torka said.

"I just thought Lord Trumma would want to know that there are those here who do not think much of his dancing, just because he has only one hind leg," Räv replied.

The bull was so angry that he tore his scented scarf in half. "Who dares say that? I can shake a leg with the best of them."

"That may be a well-known fact among our people, but . . . " Räv bit her lip.

Lord Trumma's nostrils flared elegantly. "But what, child?"

The girl glanced slyly at Lady Torka. "I wouldn't want to be accused of carrying tales."

Lord Trumma placed both forehooves upon his heart. "I simply must know who is spreading lies about me." His green skin began to glow with a soft light.

Räv glanced at Ch'ih Yu. "It's just that the windbag lord over there boasted he could outdance anyone."

Lord Trumma straightened, his nostrils swelling as he sucked in a breath. When he released it, his sides boomed like a huge kettle drum.

"I'll show him," he shouted, rumbling up from the platform like a bull charging out of a pen.

"Really, Lord Trumma, what does it matter?" Lady Torka scolded him, but the bull was speeding toward Ch'ih Yu.

"*You* aren't known as the best dancer in the seven lands," Lord Trumma said.

Lady Torka squinted her eyes in warning at Räv. "I do hope you're not playing some game, child."

The girl was the picture of innocence. "I'm only protecting our reputation."

"Are you now?" Lady Torka sniffed suspiciously, and prodded Lord Harnal. "Come, we have to stop the fool."

"But I haven't finished my desserts yet," the pig squealed in protest.

"Are you forgetting what happened the last time that bull put on a display of his dancing prowess?" Lady Torka asked.

"It took a month to repair my home." Lord Harnal sighed wearily. "Your point is well taken." His white quills clinking, he left the platform with his retinue.

The girl watched with satisfaction for a moment and then spun around clumsily. "We'd better get Junior to some place safe."

"This isn't going to break the Alliance, is it?" Tom said, suddenly afraid.

"No, because Vatten's still on the loose, but they'll have sore heads tomorrow," Räv said, floating on her back. "Pull me along, will you?"

"I thought you didn't want to be towed like a blimp," Tom said, taking her arm.

"I want to see my handiwork." She smirked, putting her hands behind her head.

"Let me see!" The phoenix tried to climb out of his pouch.

"Stay there," Tom ordered, tucking him back inside with his thumb.

Behind them, they could hear Lord Trumma bellowing out a challenge to Ch'ih Yu. "I hear you claim to be the best dancer in the palace!"

"I didn't say any such thing," Ch'ih Yu replied, tossing a handful of honey-coated pebbles into his mouth as if they were peanuts, "because I don't have to. It's known throughout the world."

Master Yen tried to act as the peacemaker. "Good sirs, please, there's no need for this."

Ch'ih Yu crunched the pebbles with loud, grating noises. "Are you saying I'm not the best dancer here?"

"No, no, Heaven forbid," Master Yen said nervously.

The thick muscles on Lord Trumma's neck swelled. "Then you're saying that *I'm* not?"

Master Yen looked from one to the other. "No, I mean, yes. I mean, no."

He was still chattering, trying to find a compromise, when Lord Trumma butted him and sent him sailing off. "Come," the bull said to Ch'ih Yu as he clopped his front hooves together rhythmically. "Name the dance. I can do anything. From the minuet to the gavotte."

Ch'ih Yu swallowed his mouthful, marble dust powdering his lips white. "What kind of warrior minces? There's only one proper dance for me—the one I created." And he began to clap his hands as he commanded the orchestra: "Strike up 'Sparks from the Anvil.'"

The pleasant tune that was playing halted abruptly, and drums and cymbals crashed together in a thunderous beat. The chimes' musicians whirled their hammers like pinwheels upon their platform.

Over his shoulder, Tom saw Ch'ih Yu jog his legs left

and right in rhythm with the tune, looking like a goat prancing in midair. Then, with a huge smile, he plunged headfirst toward Lord Trumma.

The bull, who had been watching curiously, jumped back on his single hind leg.

"Ha!" Ch'ih Yu cried triumphantly as he danced with his hands on his hips. "Made you run away."

"We'll see who flees," Lord Trumma said, annoyed. And the bull began to hop about on his leg with a surprising nimbleness.

At the climax of the chord, Lord Trumma thrust forward; and even though he only had a single hind leg, powerful muscles bulged on it, propelling him onward until his head *clong*ed against Ch'ih Yu's—which sounded remarkably empty.

"They hurt?" the phoenix asked Tom.

"No, they're . . . dancing."

The phoenix covered his ears with his wingtips. "Noisy."

"It certainly is," Tom said, cringing as the two dancers staggered back. He was glad they had left the immediate vicinity.

Lady Torka set her paws around her mouth like a megaphone so she could be heard over the music. "Enough, Lord Trumma. You've proved your point."

On the other side, Master Yen had returned and was

yelling urgently to Ch'ih Yu. "Yes, yes, exactly so."

The orchestra kept playing while the dancers' eyes came back into focus. Neither of them seemed to hear their friends as they began moving their legs again, more determined than ever to knock the other down.

By the time Tom and Räv had returned to their platform, the two dancers had banged heads several times with *clong*s and booms; and though each crash had been louder than the last, and their legs were now a little wobbly and their eyes glazed, they still kept dancing.

Mistral had a death grip on Sidney's tail. "Let me go, will you? I can make a killing taking odds," the rat said, trying to tug himself free.

"We have to stay together," Mr. Hu reprimanded.

"Where's Monkey?" Tom asked.

"While everyone was distracted, he transformed," Räv said, pulling away from Tom. "We should all be getting ready to head for the entrance."

The two dancers were now hidden by a cloud of spectators.

Almost on cue, they heard a woman shriek, "The robot's gone wild!"

Tom spun around—and had trouble stopping. He saw a winged snake careening through the crowd, scattering lords and ladies, kings and queens, as he splattered them with pastries and punch.

"Stop! What are you doing?" Master Yen said, swimming directly in front of the servant and holding up a hand. "I command you to—"

His words were choked off as a cake caught him squarely in the mouth.

"Ooh, good aim," Räv said, clapping her hands approvingly.

More cakes and custards flew into the air, thrown by the servant's unerring hand. K'ua Fu, the Dark Lady, even the Dragon King could not escape.

Mr. Hu's whiskers twitched. "Hmm, well done."

The biggest cake of all was reserved for Lady Torka. Up until then, she had been trying to restore order but stopped to honk: "You've ruined my robe!"

Mistral arched an eyebrow as she pointed at the berserk servant. "Let me guess. That's Monkey in disguise?"

Räv nodded her head and then cupped a hand behind her ear. "And any moment now . . ."

As if on cue, other voices from all around the chamber began to scream that other robots were going crazy as food flew off the trays.

"Those are the little apes throwing the food and putting the blame on the servants," she declared triumphantly.

The immediate reaction from the assembled warriors was not to flee but to attack, and they fell upon the robot servants and even upon the hapless orchestra. However, none of Master Yen's creations was easy to destroy. Winged snakes fought back with whipping tails and flapping wings, wielding trays and musical instruments as weapons.

"Ah, I see Master Yen created his servants so they could also defend his palace," Mr. Hu observed. "Except in this case, he was too clever for his own good."

Soon the chamber was a swirling chaos. Master Yen, with cake still on his face, turned first one way and then the other, unsure of where to start as he begged, "Stop, stop."

"Now," Räv said, "let's go."

The battle had become many little ones, and they had to weave their way around them and duck the debris from the robots—scraps of leather, lacquered wood, and tendons formed from gummy dragon spittle. The various retinues had also charged into the chamber to defend their masters and mistresses, adding to the confusion.

Tom kept his eyes on the swimming tiger, stopping when the Guardian stopped, dodging when he did—which was not all that easy because he had to keep one hand upon the phoenix, who was insisting he wanted to see what the commotion was about, and his other hand towed Räv. Mistral staggered as battling warriors and snake-men struck her sides.

As they fled the chamber, a chuckling Monkey settled down beside them. "I haven't had so much fun at a party in centuries."

"Don't expect to be invited back," Mistral said, bringing up the rear.

Monkey was busy transforming the little apes into hairs and then restoring these to his tail. "I didn't like the food anyway."

"You packed away plenty," Mistral said, looking all around.

"I was just testing it," Monkey said cheerfully, and somersaulted ahead.

As they followed him along the curving corridor, the palace appeared to be completely off-kilter. Sometimes the scented air was so sweet that it was almost cloying; other times it stunk as bad as a sewer. Once Tom even thought he smelled boiling cabbage. And the pearly walls of the room flexed, flashing with garish, neon colors.

"This is giving me a headache," Mr. Hu muttered.

"Not as bad as the ones Ch'ih Yu and Trumma are going to have." Räv laughed, relishing her victory.

"Where are those darn sunglasses?" Sidney began to hunt in his fur as Monkey cried out from the portal ahead: "Trouble!"

When they heard the creaking, the ape raised his staff over his shoulder. The sound grew louder and louder and then they saw Master Yen's robotic lion, which he had ridden when he came to the store.

Monkey crouched for battle, but the lion leaped over the entire group, its bright red mane flying past like fire, and landed beyond them in the corridor. Mr. Hu whirled, thinking the lion meant to attack them from the rear, but it sped away as if it were going to rescue its master.

"Phew," Sidney said, rising from behind Mistral. "That was close."

They ran out of the giant, starry portal. Below them, the earth was black wilderness. It looked like a long fall.

"A new sales territory," Sidney said, rubbing his paws together as his fur began to puff out and vibrate and he lifted into the air.

"Will you take us on your back?" Mr. Hu asked Mistral.

"I'm not sure I can carry everyone," the dragon said tensely as she flexed her wing. "I think those idiots broke some bones when they thumped against me."

"You just have to get us to the ground in one piece," Mr. Hu said.

"Oh, quit whining, Mistral," Monkey said. "I'm sure Sidney has a pot of glue to put you back together. And I'm pretty good at jigsaw puzzles."

Mr. Hu twisted his head. "Listen!" The noise in the palace had stopped.

"They must be sorting things out now," Mistral said, and she crouched so Tom could climb onto her shoulders.

Räv and Mr. Hu clambered up behind the boy.

Tom whispered to the phoenix, "Stay inside now." Despite the little bird's protests, he pulled the drawstrings so that the mouth closed over the chick's head.

"There's rarely a dull moment around you, Hu, old boy," Monkey said, and hopped off toward the dark world below.

CHAPTER EIGHT

As they fell out of the palace, the rush of air nearly tore Tom from Mistral's back, and desperately he wrapped his arms around her neck, pressing his face tightly against her scales. He just hoped Räv and Mr. Hu, both behind him, had as tight a grip as he did.

Tom barely heard the phoenix's shrill protest. "Mama, you squeeze me."

He tried to soothe the frightened bird. "Shh, it'll be over soon."

"One way or another," Räv moaned.

Tom felt Mistral's powerful muscles fighting to spread her wings like giant leathery sails, but she could only maneuver with her uninjured left wing and they began to corkscrew downward. The wind, created as the dragon fell, came even closer to knocking her riders off.

Sidney was a furry balloon on their left. "Pull up! Pull up!"

Monkey somersaulted next to them on their right. "We're not done feuding yet, you overgrown lizard."

"Shut up, both of you," puffed Mistral.

Tom risked a glance downward. The earth seemed like a blackness into which they could fall forever.

"I know you can do it," he encouraged his friend. "There's too much depending on us. Think of Ring Neck." Ring Neck had given his life to let them escape the dragon kingdom.

The dragon didn't answer, but she fought even harder; with an agonized groan she unfurled her right wing and they began to glide forward.

Straining his eyes, Tom could make out the shoulders of the mountain range outlined dimly by the moon. They were already passing over its foothills. A river, reflecting the faint light, shone like a silver ribbon and the image of a struggling dragon rippled on the surface.

Mistral's reflection rippled again as she sought to flap her great wings. Once, twice, she succeeded. And then there was a sickening crack, like a tree branch breaking.

"My wing," she screamed.

Tom saw that her right wing was hanging at an unnatural angle. Helplessly, they spiraled downward again, whirling around even faster.

Tom did his best to hold on, but he felt himself being

107

whipped off. For a moment, he saw the stars of the night sky. If it were not for the wind, he could pretend he was back in the sea watching the star rise; but strangely there was no sign of the Sky Palace itself. Master Yen must have made his palace invisible so that it could float unobserved in the night.

"Mama, Mama!" the phoenix screamed.

"I'm sorry," he said, cupping a hand over the pouch. He tried to twist protectively so his back was to the ground and could cushion the bird, even though he knew that would ultimately be useless.

Tom was surprised when he hit, for though the landing knocked the breath out of him, he felt himself falling into a cold, dark wetness. For a moment he was disoriented, but then he saw a shining disk above him. Instinctively, he kicked toward it and found himself breaking out of the water.

By the light of the moon, he could see he was on the surface of a lake. He put a hand to his pouch. "Are you all right?"

To his immense relief, a damp red head poked out. "Wet," complained the little bird as Tom tread water to keep them afloat.

From the splashing nearby, he knew that the others had also landed in the water. "Mr. Hu?" he called.

"I'm here, but I can't find Räv," the Guardian answered. "She can't swim!"

"We got her," Monkey said from his right. Tom turned to see Monkey and Sidney hovering, each holding on to a wrist of the coughing girl and keeping her head above water.

"What about Mistral?" Tom asked.

He saw the dark bulk of the dragon, floating half out of the water. They all converged on their friend, but Mr. Hu, who was closest, held a paw before her nostrils. "She's still breathing, but I think she's passed out from the pain."

"Well, she's used to living underwater, so at least she can't drown. Let's get the children to the shore and figure out what to do," Monkey said.

The moonlight shone from the ripples of their wake as they headed toward the dark land. It sounded like they were moving toward an army, but then Tom realized the rustling was from the trees that crowded against the lake. Gratefully he felt the pebbly slope at last beneath his feet.

"I'll go the rest of the way on my own," Räv spluttered. She jerked her hands free so hard that she nearly banged Monkey and Sidney together in a midair collision. Her silvery hair was plastered to her head like a helmet, and dripping water from her clothes, she stumbled up onto the shore, where she fell on her knees. "From now on, I never want to stand any higher than on top of a chair," she gasped.

Tom was stiff from the chill and wet, and his body ached from the fall, but he cupped his hands around the shivering bird to try to warm it. Then he shuffled over toward the elderly tiger, who was on all fours. "Oh, how I loathe water," the Guardian said, shaking himself like a dog and showering his apprentice with water.

"They'll see Mistral," Tom said, pointing at the sky. Far overhead they could see Lady Torka and a flock of winged foxes. The unconscious dragon's dark shape still floated in the lake.

The soggy tiger quickly began to mutter a spell, his paws weaving intricate designs in the air. "There. I've cast an illusion. From a distance, they should mistake her for a small island."

Other creatures were also searching for them, swarming out of what looked like an empty patch in the evening sky and flitting by like fireflies far above.

Räv sneezed and Tom was so cold he had to grit his teeth to keep them from chattering.

"Mama, Papa, all right?" the phoenix asked.

"Come to me, children," Mr. Hu called. Tom and Räv huddled next to him. Despite his wet clothes and fur, the tiger felt as hot as a furnace.

"Doggy is cold," the phoenix said, for Sidney's teeth were chattering.

"You too, Sidney," Mr. Hu said, and the rat gratefully scampered to get his share of the tiger's warmth.

"Doggy, you feel better?"

As he pressed against Mr. Hu, Sidney said, "Yeah.

Thanks. So how about compromising? Call me *Uncle Doggy*."

"Uncle Doggy," the phoenix agreed.

After a while, Monkey announced, "The sky's clear."

Tom looked around the steep, forested slope, where the pine trees stirred restlessly. "Is this really China? On television, they always show shots of cities and factories."

"It's a big country," Mr. Hu explained, "and there are many parts that the human hand has touched only lightly." He motioned to the rat. "Sidney, do you have any rope? We really can't have Mistral floating out there like a big rubber duck. We'll pull her to shore. And the exercise will warm us up."

"I just have clothesline," the rat said. "I don't think it'll be strong enough."

"It will have to do," the tiger replied.

At Mr. Hu's instructions, Monkey flew out to Mistral and tied the line to one of her legs before he flew back. Passing it around a tree, they all began to pull, slowly hauling the inert dragon until she lay half in and half out of the water like a beached whale.

"Let's tend to her wing, if we can," Mr. Hu said.

For splints, Monkey broke off branches and Tom and Räv trimmed them with a knife borrowed from Sidney.

Mr. Hu had just finished binding the splints to her wing with sections of rope when the dragon gave a groan and moved her head, rubbing her cheek against the shore.

111

The tiger lightly leaped down from her side to land near her head. "Easy, old friend. You've had a nasty fall."

"Did anybody get hurt?" was Mistral's first question.

Monkey squatted down next to Mr. Hu. "Only you. You really have to work on your landings, dear girl."

Mistral shut her eyes. "Why don't I practice dropping on top of your head."

"She's back to her old self," Monkey said, relieved.

Mr. Hu placed a paw upon her neck. "Can you crawl under the trees? We have to get you out of sight before the sun rises."

"I think I can." She winced as she rolled onto her belly and then rose on all fours, crawling up the gentle slope until she was under the trees.

With a branch in his paw, Monkey went back to erase their tracks while the others huddled around the dragon.

"Thank you," Tom said to her.

"You didn't do half-bad," Räv added.

"A compliment from the ambassador. Now I can die happy," Mistral said, closing her eyes.

"Pretty," the phoenix said, gazing up at the night sky.

"Those are stars," Tom explained, "just like the crystal one you saw in Chinatown."

"So many." The little bird stared, awestruck, until he suddenly sneezed.

Tom wrapped his hands around the trembling creature. "He's getting cold. We need a fire."

"Perhaps we can look for a cave," Monkey said.
"Let me help in the meantime."

Much to Tom's surprise, Räv rose to her knees and covered Tom's hands with her own, adding her warmth.

Monkey stood. "I'll—"

He stopped when they heard an angry bellow from farther up the wooded slope.

CHAPTER NINE

Rat and Bird
On a mountain with much white jade, there are rats and birds who live together in burrows. The rat has a short tail and stays at home digging while the bird stays outside. The bird is small with yellow and black feathers.

The Chu Huai
Beware if you see an ox with four horns but with eyes like a man's and ears like a pig's and it honks like a goose. It eats human flesh.

Pi Fang
There is a bird that looks like a crane with a single leg. It has a body that is gray-green with red stripes and its beak is a snowy white. A strange, cold, glowing light appears in its wake.

—Shan Hai Ching

Mr. Hu turned, golden eyes gleaming and nostrils twitching as he surveyed the trees and sorted through the scents. "This way. The children and Sidney in the middle. Monkey, you protect them. Mistral, protect the rear."

"Here we go again." Sidney sighed. A silver spoon tinkled on the ground as he extracted a hatchet from his fur.

"Just how many souvenirs are you carrying?" Monkey asked, taking the needle from behind his ear and transforming it into his ringed staff.

"When you have a lot of fun, you need a lot of mementos." The rat shrugged.

They went with as much speed as they could into the dark woods, where the trees shut out most of the moonlight. With his keen eyes, Mr. Hu slipped silently through the brush, and Tom found that his tiger's blood let him see a bit better than Räv, who frequently blundered into shrubs.

Tom turned to her, and he could almost feel the amber flecks glowing in his eyes. "I'll go first," he whispered, and he felt her grasp the back of his robe.

The ground sloped up sharply as they climbed away from the river toward the bellowing and yelling.

"Take that and that and that," a voice was shouting.

"And that and that and that," a high voice twittered.

"Halt," Mr. Hu whispered to Tom behind him, who passed the word to the others. Mistral crept up beside them on the right, head and belly low to the ground so that she slithered like a snake. Monkey crawled to their left side with Räv and Sidney.

Raising a claw to his lip, Mr. Hu pointed in front of them. "*Chu huai*," he murmured to his apprentice.

Carefully Tom parted the shrub in front of him and

115

saw in the moonlit clearing a half-dozen creatures built like massive oxen but with two pairs of wicked horns thrusting from their heads. The horn tips had been sheathed in iron to make them even deadlier weapons. Their ears were long and floppy like a pig's and their eyes were strangely human, and each creature bore a violet tattoo of a 9 with a serpent's tail. Around the shoulders of one was a blue cloak.

Sidney spoke for everyone when he said softly, "Now, there's some big bruisers."

One of them easily looked like a match for Mr. Hu or Monkey, and a pair of them might even give the dragon a hard time.

"They were some of Vatten's deadliest warriors," Räv said. "I hear they stayed loyal to him. He always used them as his shock troops, surprising the enemy and breaking down their first line of defense."

"And now that Vatten's not controlling them, they've turned into bandits," Monkey whispered.

Standing on their hind legs, four oxlike creatures were loading baskets from one of the small caves in the cliff face onto the back of a huge two-wheeled cart where a fifth creature in a cloak waited. In front of the cart was the oddest bird. It was tall and lean as a crane, but it stood only upon one red-striped leg. Its feathers were a grayish green, and its beak cloud white, with its scarlet nostrils standing out in contrast like burning coals. A glowing yellow light surrounded it, stirring like a cloud whenever it moved.

"I thought all the *pi fangs* had disappeared from this world," Mr. Hu murmured as he studied the bird.

A sixth chu huai was holding off the apparent owners of the baskets, a small yellow-and-black bird and a gray rat of about the same size, who was swinging an ornately carved club. Though the chu huai stomped his hooves and thrust his horns and swung his huge axe, both bird and rat were too nimble for him; and every time they struck him with beak or club, the monster bellowed.

"Thieves, knaves," the yellow-and-black bird was shouting as she flitted here and there.

"Give us back our food," the gray rat hollered as it dashed and dodged the hooves and axe.

The frustrated chu huai turned to his fellows. "Give me a hand killing these two."

The cloaked chu huai seemed to be the leader, because he signed to the others to do just that; each of the four picked up an axe from where they leaned against the side of the cart.

Tom could feel his blood stirring as he drew his lips back in a snarl.

"I think we should even up the odds," Mistral said.

Mr. Hu's ears flattened against his skull and his eyes narrowed. "So do I."

"Wait," Monkey said. Sitting up, he began to pull hairs from his tail.

"What can your little apes do against those monsters?" Mistral demanded. "Their hides are like armor."

Mr. Hu touched Mistral's shoulder to silence her. "Let them go. At the very least, they'll distract the chu huai."

For an instant, Monkey's head was hidden in a cloud of little apes flitting around like flies. In the clearing, one of the oxlike creatures paused. His floppy ears rose as he turned toward them suspiciously.

"He's heard us," Mistral said, rising from her belly.

"Go, children," Monkey ordered, and the little apes, separating into six flocks, darted off.

"Master Thomas, you stay here with Mistress Räv and Sidney," Mr. Hu said sternly.

Tom had to fight the tiger's blood surging through his body, but he knew his master was right and nodded his obedience.

"Kamsin!" Mistral roared as she leaped into the clearing, and the tiger sprang after her.

"Wait, let my children do their work!" Monkey called to his friends, and then, as they continued charging, he threw his hat down. "Those two never listen to me." With an exasperated click of his tongue, the ape bounced out of the brush. "Well, I'd better go save them."

As the chu huai bellowed angrily, Räv slipped the stiletto from her wrist sheath. She looked at it doubtfully. "I don't know how much harm this could do against one of those monsters."

Sidney had his hatchet in both paws, but he seemed relieved that he was staying behind. "I'd want a cannon at least."

"And," Tom said, "even that may not be enough." Now that he had a moment, he tried to turn his fury to something constructive. His fists could do little damage to these monsters, but perhaps his spells might.

Though the chu huai were surprised by the attack, they recovered quickly. They were Vatten's best warriors, and they proved it. The chu huai pivoted to meet the new attackers.

"Go on," Mr. Hu snarled to Mistral and Monkey as he struck at one of the chu huai. Tom gasped as the tiger hopped to the side, narrowly avoiding being gored.

"No hurt," the phoenix cried, peeking out of his pouch.

"Stay down," Tom ordered, and he used his thumb to shove the little bird out of sight.

Monkey barely managed to avoid being chopped in half by an axe blade swung by a second chu huai, and the other four converged on Mistral from different sides.

"They're trying to kill the strongest first," Räv grunted. "They may know only one thing, but that's fighting."

Monkey's iron staff rang against his opponent's axe. Though the weapon had a long shaft and huge metal head, the chu huai handled it as if it were no heavier than a sheet of paper; with his greater reach and longer weapon, he was able to keep Monkey from getting in close enough to land a blow.

The noise upset the phoenix. "No hurt, no hurt," he kept whimpering.

Tom could feel him against his chest, shivering with fright. He covered the cowering bird. It felt so small and fragile against his palm. "I won't let anything hurt you," he promised, though he was not sure how he could keep that vow—he wasn't sure who would win.

Mr. Hu's suit, vest, and shirt had already been torn and Tom thought he saw red on the tiger's belly; but his enemy had also paid with long slash marks on his flanks. Mistral had not waited to be attacked; hoping to reduce the odds with a quick victory, she had plunged at the one in front of her, swinging her tail wildly back and forth to keep the others away. However, the chu huai was as quick as he was big and he fell back.

Suddenly, the heads of the chu huai were hidden in clouds of little apes. Each warrior stiffened and their bellows were choked off as little apes invaded nostrils and throats and poked at eyes.

Finally, Monkey got in close to his enemy and knocked him out with a blow of his staff. Mr. Hu dispatched his the next second. Mistral had already tossed an injured chu huai to the ground and was swinging around to take out the others.

"One of them's escaping," Räv said in surprise, as the

cloaked chu huai picked up two slender threads that were barely visible at this distance; but as they drew closer, they saw that these threads were connected like reins to a string bridle on the pi fang's head.

The bird unfolded its great wings and shook them, sending ripples of light dancing around the clearing. Then, with a hop of its one leg and a dirt-scattering flap, it rose into the air, tugging the cart up behind it.

Both the rat and bird looked so thin and bedraggled that Tom suspected they desperately needed their food stores. "We can't let him do that."

Sidney looked frightened, but his fur began to billow and a humming sound filled the air. "I guess it's up to me then," he said, gripping his hatchet grimly.

Frantic with fear, the phoenix had poked his head from the pouch. "No hurt!" His hysterical voice rose shrilly.

Tom didn't think anyone at that distance would hear, but the pi fang swung its head around. "Your Highness," the pi fang called.

"The phoenix," bellowed the chu huai eagerly. The monster yanked at the reins and the pi fang banked into a sharp dive.

As the monster bore down on them, Sidney said, "Well, here goes nothing."

Before the rat could rise very high, Tom had caught hold of a hind paw. "Wait. Let me try something."

Crouching, Tom began to snarl the wind spell to knock the chu huai from the cart; but before he could finish, he heard the phoenix cry shrilly, "No hurt!"

The cart crashed so hard against the ground that it was amazing it didn't break; but the only thing that came off was the driver, who went flying to the side. The pi fang landed with a hop and a skip, bouncing along on its one leg as it kept ahead of the sturdy cart.

Räv crumpled to her knees, holding her head, while Sidney began to zigzag through the air like a drunken bumblebee. In the clearing, the combatants collapsed in heaps.

The pi fang dropped to the ground. Fortunately for the bird, the cart had lost most of its momentum and simply bumped it.

"No hurt," the phoenix crowed proudly.

"What did you do?" Tom asked as he knelt beside Räv.

"I stop fight," the phoenix said. "Mama says no hurt."

"Are you all right?" Tom helped Räv to sit up.

Only gibberish came from her lips and her eyes were as blank and innocent as a newborn baby's. Sidney was hovering, sampling dead leaves and pebbles in his paw like a toddler. Mr. Hu was trying to catch his wriggling tail.

In the clearing, the former enemies had all sat up and were giggling and playing with one another like children. The pi fang opened its beak and squawked like a newly hatched chick, as did the yellow-and-black bird. Her companion, the gray rat, had dropped his club and was busy chasing a floating feather.

"You've turned them into kids." Tom gaped. "How did you do that?"

"I not know." The phoenix shrugged. "I just do it."

"Can you undo it?"

The phoenix closed one eye as it strained in thought. "I guess so."

"Then undo our friends."

"They'll fight again." The bird pouted.

"Not if you leave the big monsters like children," Tom said. He pointed to Räv. "Now listen to your mama. Papa's not right in the head."

"I guess," the phoenix admitted after studying the girl for a moment.

"If you leave her and our friends like that, we can't be a family anymore," Tom said.

"No?"

"No," Tom insisted. "So change her and our friends back." When the chick still hesitated, he added, "Please."

"Oh, all right." The phoenix took a deep breath and shut its eyes tightly.

The next moment, Räv put a hand to her head. "What happened? I have such a headache."

Sidney landed on his haunches, searching through his

fur. "Me too. Where's my aspirin?"

Tom pointed at the pi fang and then the little gray rat and bird. "Them too."

When the phoenix was done, he turned his large eyes toward Tom. "I did good."

"Yes, you did," Tom said, and got up to help the others. "See to them, will you, Sidney?" He nodded at the chu huai's victims, who were still recovering. Then he and Räv went to help their friends, dodging around the chu huai who were now childishly butting heads together.

"No hurt," the phoenix warned them as Tom and he passed.

"They're just playing," Tom said—though with creatures as large as the chu huai, their games were dangerous enough to themselves and to bystanders. This close, Tom could see their bulging muscles and the sharpness of their horns. He was glad he had not had to face one on his own.

He noticed Räv was examining the bellowing chu huai. "What are you doing?" he asked her.

"Seeing if there are any orders or maps," she said, plucking at the pouches strapped to their chests.

The pi fang struggled to its foot and bowed so low it almost lost its balance. "Your Highness."

"Hello," the phoenix said, emerging from his pouch. The pi fang followed him attentively as Tom went to each of his friends. All were still groggy and had pain in their heads. Tom dispensed some of Sidney's aspirin to Monkey and to Mr. Hu and then the rest to the dragon, who was lying, clutching her head and groaning.

As Tom helped the elderly Guardian, he was relieved to see the tiger had received only a shallow gash. But suddenly he felt ashamed. "It was the phoenix," Tom confessed. "He—"

"I know," Mr. Hu said gently. "Now you understand his power, Master Thomas. A more mature phoenix could control it better. But a young one cannot."

"How wide could his powers reach?" Tom asked as he began to tear strips from his robe.

"Legend says it could be the whole world," Mr. Hu said, massaging his temples.

"It's worse than an atom bomb?"

"Yes, in the wrong hands, the phoenix is the ultimate weapon." The tiger watched as the pi fang knelt before the phoenix. "That's why he can never be used. That's why the Guardians were created."

Tom glanced down in awe at the phoenix, who was touching beaks with the pi fang. Next to the large bird, the chick seemed like a ball of fluff. And yet this small creature could wreak more havoc than any army. And it was up to him to guide this awesome power. It left Tom feeling humble—and scared, not only for his tiny child but for himself as well. What if he failed in his duty?

"So we'd better keep him away from Vatten," Mistral said, lying on her side to inspect her wounds.

"He should be kept away from everybody," Tom said. "I think I'm beginning to understand."

"He cannot even be used by *us*," Mr. Hu emphasized as Tom helped him off with his coat, "no matter how excellent our reasons might be. We might appear to do good at first, but once we started using his power, we couldn't resist doing it again and again—until in the end the power would corrupt us and we would become as evil as Vatten."

Mistral used her tail to guide the playful chu huai away from her. "Still, if he had done this earlier, he could have saved us all some pain."

Monkey laid down his staff and began changing the little apes back to hairs and restoring them to his tail. "If *you*'d waited, we would have had an easier time. But you had to charge in before my children could do their work."

Mistral watched the chu huai trot off into the bushes. "How could I know your strategy would work, attacking their faces with your little monkeys?"

"Did you ever stop to think why farmers can lead bulls around by the rings in their noses?" Monkey tapped his nostrils. "The flesh is soft inside, so it's sensitive to pain."

"It's imperative that His Highness reach the Imperfect Mountain," Mr. Hu said to the pi fang. "Will you take us?"

The pi fang's head bobbed up and down. "Anything for His Highness."

"We aren't thieves," Mistral called to Räv, who was

picking the pouch of the cloaked chu huai.

"I was looking for information," the girl said indignantly.

Mistral waggled a claw for her to turn around. "Is that what's in your hand?"

"I was going to put the gold nuggets back in his pouch," Räv snapped, throwing them on the ground.

"She looked so innocent when she was under the phoenix's spell," Tom muttered to the tiger as he helped him sit upon a basket. "Maybe I should have left her that way."

"It's tempting," the tiger agreed.

As their group prepared to leave, they saw that the chu huai seemed to have begun a game of tag in the forest, and their leader was "it." Shedding his cloak, he ran after them, bellowing happily.

CHAPTER TEN

The yellow-and-black bird was still shaking her head groggily, and Mr. Hu bent over her kindly. "Are you all right?"

"Get away from her!" a shrill voice cried. Her companion, the gray rat, had already recovered and was charging toward Mr. Hu, waving the club over his head. "I'm warning you. I may be small but I'm the terror of the mountains."

Trying not to laugh, Mr. Hu rose and stepped back. "I have no doubt about that," he said.

Sidney helped the bird up. "Relax, cuz. We're on your side. We helped drive away the bad guys."

The bird fluttered over in alarm to her defender. "Please, Master Thick. Restrain yourself! The thieves are gone. And these visitors don't look like the rowdy sort."

Master Thick gave a snort. "A tiger, a dragon, a monkey,

a rat, and a pair of humans. I can't think of anything more suspicious." The rat brandished his club over his head. "Be off with you or I'll send the lot of you packing!"

The bird settled to the ground and put her wing around the gray rat to hold him back as she apologized to Mr. Hu and his friends. "Please don't be frightened. My husband has such a temper when my safety is involved."

"Let me go, Mistress Quick," the gray rat said, trying to pull free. "My blood's aboil."

"No hurt!" the phoenix shouted from his pouch, and Tom looked down, afraid the bird might use his power again.

Sidney ducked behind the nearest shrub so that only his voice could be heard from behind the squat bush. "That's right. We're all just one happy family here."

Tom noticed that even the dragon had taken care to keep her distance from the chick.

The little bird began chanting, "No hurt, no hurt, no hurt."

It wasn't the Guardian who had been spared the phoenix's recent display of power. Nor was it the Guardian whom the little bird called Mama. Tom felt the full weight of his responsibility come crashing down upon him: *Through his child, he could remake the world the way he thought it should be.* He didn't want to take it over like Vatten, but he could correct all the bad things. The power made him feel giddy for a moment. It was one thing for Mr.

Hu to lecture about it but another thing to experience it.

Even now, the phoenix regarded him intently. No one had ever paid attention to Tom like the little bird did. In the chick's eyes was such love, such trust.

He didn't feel worthy of such admiration. There were far better people to whom the phoenix should listen, but chance had brought them together. In the back of his mind, he could hear his grandmother whispering to him, "You can only try to match what your loved ones think of you and the results may surprise you."

And the temptation passed. How could he be sure if he was really correcting things or only making them worse?

Tom lifted the phoenix in his pouch. "I told you it was wrong to hurt someone. When you use your power, it's worse than any hurt."

The little bird argued sullenly, "They fight. That more wrong."

Tom rubbed his head. The Guardians had existed for millennia. But how could he explain the principle to such a young chick? "You're right, it was wrong for them to fight; but that's what they chose to do. When you force someone to do something against their will, that's worse than any fighting."

The phoenix's feathers puffed out in an angry red explosion. "I hurt no one. I stop hurt. I is king. You listen to me!"

The little bird looked so resentful that Tom wondered if he was going to be blasted now; but he couldn't let such a powerful creature run wild. Licking his lips, he said, "Just because you're a king doesn't mean you can do whatever you want."

The phoenix wriggled in the pouch. "Yes, I can! Yes, I can!"

Tom did the craziest, bravest thing he had ever done—crazier and braver even than when the phoenix was an egg and he had run into the Watcher's lair to recover it, nearly getting himself killed. Lifting the phoenix so he could look directly at him, Tom said, "No."

He heard the others gasp around him.

"Let me go!" The phoenix squirmed furiously in his fingers.

"Listen to me," Tom said urgently.

The little bird turned angry eyes, round and black as stones, toward him so that Tom saw his own frightened image reflected in them.

"Do you love Mama?" Tom asked.

He had an anxious moment while the phoenix paused.

"Mama love me?" the little bird demanded.

"Yes," Tom said, and he meant it. "Yes, I do," he said, nodding his head for emphasis.

"I love Mama," the little bird said.

Tom almost sighed with relief, but he knew it was too

soon. "Then you have to trust me. I know you don't understand, but you can't use your power."

"Not ever?" the phoenix asked, puzzled.

"Not unless I tell you it's okay," Tom said.

For a moment, Tom wondered if he was going to bring the entire Guardianship crashing down; but the phoenix chirped, "Okay, Mama."

Tom's legs gave out from underneath him and he knelt on the ground. "And do you love Papa?"

"Sure," the phoenix assured him. "We is family."

"Well, you can't ever do what you did to her . . . I mean, him, I mean, her." Tom gave up and simply jerked his head at Räv. "I mean Papa."

"Okay," the little bird said.

"And Mistral."

"Okay."

"And what about dear old Uncle Sidney, who promises to read you lots and lots of bedtime stories when we get home," the rat called from behind his shrub.

The phoenix looked at Tom, and when he nodded, the little bird chirped, "Okay, Uncle Doggy."

After that, it was easy to get the little bird to promise not to use his power on Grandpa Hu and Uncle Monkey.

Mistral strolled over. "We might want to rethink that one about the ape."

"Everyone in our *family*," Tom insisted.

The dragon regarded him with amusement. "You've grown, boy." She dipped her head in acknowledgment. "Very well. Just as you say."

Now Mistress Quick hovered before Tom and the phoenix. "Your Highness!" she gasped.

Mr. Hu was quick to pick up on that. "Yes, we are the escort for your king."

The bird suddenly became all flustered, glancing down at her ruffled feathers. "Oh . . . I had no idea. . . . And me in such disrepair."

"That's all right," Mr. Hu said more kindly. "But you can see we mean you no harm, can't you?"

The yellow-and-black bird settled down beside her husband. "Ah, yes. Let me compose myself. Master Thick, guess what? We have royal visitors." She waved a wing at Tom and the phoenix. "Behold the King of All Birds. And these are his . . . um . . . family?"

"Oh, well, fancy that," the gray rat said, twitching his tail.

"They're city folk," she said with a worldly wink, "and you know how different their ways can be."

"There's different and then there's different," Master Thick muttered, scratching his head. "Anyway, sorry, Your Highness, but you can't be too careful."

Mistress Quick tenderly brushed her husband's head with a wing. "There are such disreputable people passing

133

through our mountains nowadays."

"Like the chu huai," Mr. Hu said.

"Is that what those thieves call themselves? Hereabouts we just call them the rowdies." Master Thick shrugged. "Aye, and there's uglier ones than them too."

Mistress Quick sniffed. "Everyone in the mountains is complaining about them. They came in a week ago and started grabbing all the food and bullying everyone terribly."

Even by moonlight, the others could see how scrawny and bedraggled the bird and rat were. The recent invasions seemed to have taken their toll on the couple.

"It sounds like more than banditry," Mr. Hu said.

The ape nodded. "It sounds like an army gathering up supplies. Do you think Vatten's getting ready to attack the mountain?"

"Before the battle in Chinatown, he could have given them a rendezvous point in the event of a setback," the tiger replied. "They were probably supposed to scatter into small bands and make their way there."

"Then it's even more important we get to the mountain," Mistral said grimly.

"Well, the rowdies made a big mistake when they tried to steal our food!" Master Thick said, waving his club again.

Mistress Quick put a wing on his paw and forced the club back down. "Master Thick, you really must calm down.

134

Every time you get excited, it upsets your stomach so."

Master Thick tapped his club against the dirt. "Aye, it's a curse to have this much strength and such a tender belly."

Sidney pulled a bottle of tonic from his fur. "I got just the tonic for you, cousin." He set it down. "The first bottle's free."

In the pouch, the phoenix gave a sniff and Tom could feel him beginning to shiver. "We have to get Jun—I mean, His Highness, to someplace warm."

Mistress Quick clapped a wing to her forehead. "How thoughtless of me. Please, our homes are your homes."

"Homes?" Räv asked, looking around. All they could see were dozens of identical holes dug into the cliff faces.

"My wife is the envy of every homemaker in the mountains," Master Thick boasted.

She took to the air in her proud eagerness and fluttered about. "It may not be a palace like His Highness's, but I trust he'll find it comfy enough."

Mistral stared dubiously at the cliff. "I doubt if any would be big enough for me."

Master Thick studied the dragon. "I think you'd fit into the Harvest Hole."

"My husband dug that one in the month of the Harvest Moon," Mistress Quick explained.

As it turned out, all the holes were named after

months or even years. "My wife always keeps me busy digging a new home," Master Thick declared.

Mistress Quick gave a polite cough. "I'm famous for my décor. To keep up with the changes in fashion, one must move forward."

The phoenix sneezed, and Tom asked worriedly, "Do you have one that's warm?"

"Yes, right this way," the yellow-and-black bird said eagerly.

"Is it big?" the phoenix asked. "Mama and Papa sleep there too."

"We can't sleep together," Räv objected, gesturing at Tom.

"We is family," the phoenix said stubbornly.

When he saw Mistress Quick's confusion, Tom said hastily, "Papa snores. It's better if she . . . he sleeps separate."

"But I'll be right next door, where I can protect you," Räv promised.

The yellow-and-black bird kept her husband running about, fetching things. Soon she had the phoenix wrapped in a blanket woven from plant fibers that she had colorfully dyed; he lay down upon a bed of fragrant herbs and leaves where he soon fell asleep, exhausted by the first use of his power.

The rest of them ate outside, making a meal out of

some of Sidney's loot from the palace, which he had stored in his fur. The food was served in bowls of soft wood that Mistress Quick had carved herself with various pastoral scenes of farmers and water buffalo and flocks of ducks. The loyal pi fang took his meal just outside the phoenix's burrow.

Though Mistress Quick ate with ladylike pecks, it was plain she was starved. Master Thick ate with much less decorum, wolfing down everything he could; but between swallows, he kept assuring her that it was nothing compared to her cooking. Tom, who had positioned himself so that he could keep an eye on the phoenix's burrow, had set aside a slice of cake for the little bird's meal when he woke up.

When everyone had eaten their fill, Mr. Hu turned to their hosts. "I wonder if you could tell me how we can reach the Imperfect Mountain?"

Master Thick exchanged a startled look with his wife. "Well, it'd be seven days as the the bird flies. But why would anyone go into that wasteland?"

"We have an important errand there," Mr. Hu said firmly.

Mistress Quick crouched, touching her head and beak to the dirt. "Whatever the rest of you do, I beg you not to take His Highness there."

"We don't dare leave him here with all the 'rowdies'

about," Mr. Hu said, gently nudging her upright. "It's vital we reach it."

"You're set in your minds, are you?" Master Thick asked.

"We are," Mr. Hu rumbled.

Mistress Quick was so agitated that she began to hop about. "Oh, Master Thick, don't let them go!"

The gray rat draped a foreleg around his wife. "Heaven would never let harm come to such a dear little thing. Someone will watch over them."

At Mr. Hu's request, their host drew a map in the dirt. "You'll have to follow the ridgeline," Master Thick said, drawing a wavering line and then another line slashing across it. "From what my wife's kin tell me, you'll eventually reach a pass. Then you have to cross a desert wasteland, but you should be able to see the Imperfect Mountain sticking up like a big stump."

Mistral pondered the map. "Vatten's monsters might be heading to that same pass."

"Then we'd better get there before them," Monkey said.

"I doubt I can fly with this wing," Mistral said, wincing as she tried to flex it.

"Mr. Hu can change the rest of us into dragons," Tom suggested, "and we can carry you there."

The Guardian shook his head. "I have to save my

strength for Vatten. We'll have to ride in the pi fang's cart. But tomorrow, after we've rested."

After they had returned the precious stores to a hole that Mistress Quick called "the pantry," she escorted them to other burrows of all sizes, reflecting the changes in her decorating tastes. The Harvest Hole proved more than large enough for the dragon—though it took a bit of squeezing to get her through the tunnel.

Monkey gave a cough. "You'd have an easier time getting inside if you shrink."

Mistral's voice was muffled by the tunnel, but her indignation was clear. "A dragon must be of a proper size at all times, you furbag." Dirt and gravel flew as her hind paws dug at the ground so she could pop inside.

"The real adventure for her will be getting out," Monkey said, and nudged Sidney. "Too bad you can't sell tickets to see that."

Sidney turned out to be the finicky one, insisting on inspecting the remaining burrows. As they showed him one hole after another, Mistress Quick could not have been more patient—perhaps because it also gave her an opportunity to show off all her work. It finally dawned on Tom that the enterprising rat was not selecting a bed for the night but inspecting Mistress Quick's furnishings and decorations for possible later business.

While Monkey went back to erase their tracks, the kindly bird and rat settled each of their guests in his or her burrow, making beds of fresh-cut pine branches and then heaping dried fragrant leaves and flowers over everyone to keep them warm.

When Monkey returned, Mr. Hu told him that he would keep the first watch.

"I'm too awake," Monkey said. "Why don't we exchange?"

The tiger yawned. "That might be a good idea. I'm having trouble keeping my eyes open."

As Mr. Hu padded off to his burrow, Monkey selected a spot under a tree whose drooping branches would hide him from sight. He had no sooner sat down when his head received a terrific thump.

"Ha!" Master Thick cried, and was most apologetic when Monkey turned around. "Begging your pardon, Master Monkey. I didn't recognize you at first."

"It's annoying how often that happens," Monkey said, rubbing his skull.

"If you're too scared to sleep, you needn't be." Master Thick tapped his ornate club against a paw. "*I'll* see to it that you and the king are safe while you're with me."

Monkey was glad that the darkness hid his smile. "I thank you for that, Master Thick, but perhaps I'll keep you company for a while."

"Suit yourself then," Master Thick said, sitting down beside the ape.

To pass the time, the gray rat began to whittle a branch with his sharp teeth. Since he felt he was more than enough protection, it never occurred to him to wonder why his guests woke up in turns to sit beside him. He only observed later to his wife that they were nice enough folk but terribly restless.

CHAPTER ELEVEN

The Chiang Ling
They have human bodies but their limbs are long and their heads
are like a tiger's. Their tongues and hands wriggle like serpents.
—Shan Hai Ching

True to Monkey's prediction, it took Mistral twice as long to exit her burrow the next morning as it had taken to enter. As they got ready to climb onto the pi fang's cart, Mistress Quick presented a huge bouquet of flowers as well as a small sack of seeds to the phoenix. "I thought His Highness might like this. I wish the bag could be as big as the bouquet, but it should help when you feel a little peckish."

Thinking of their meager supplies, Tom knew what a sacrifice this was. "Thank you, but we can't accept this."

"It my gift," the phoenix said, annoyed. "Mama take."

Mr. Hu cleared his throat. "It's all right, Master Thomas. Knowing when to accept a present is as important as knowing when to give one." Tom reluctantly took the seeds.

"Thank you," Tom said, and then he nudged the phoenix, who added his thanks as well.

Still worried about their journey into the wasteland, Mistress Quick began to weep so much that she could barely speak. "You're welcome."

Between comforting pats on his wife's back, Master Thick was more practical, presenting Tom and Räv with stout clubs he had whittled the night before. "You're only humans—no offense meant. Live and let live I always say, but you'll need these, since you don't have fangs or claws. I'm sorry there wasn't time to prettify them, but I managed this much."

Räv looked at hers with a laugh. On it was carved the word *please*. On Tom's were the words *thank you*.

Their host drew himself up. "Remember those words, and they'll carry you far," he advised solemnly.

Tom was not sure he would ever use the club, but he made a point of thanking his host as he tucked it into the silk cord that served as his robe's belt.

Mistress Quick was now sobbing so heavily that she had developed a hiccough and could only wave a wing in farewell.

"Heaven speed you on your way," Master Thick wished them, looking almost as troubled as his wife. "And don't forget, children," he said, brandishing his own club over his head, "if *please* and *thank you* don't work, there's nothing like a good thump with a club to make someone remember their manners."

This was followed by a slight delay when Mistral, who

could not fly yet, was informed she would have to shrink in order to fit into the cart and the proud dragon resisted. However, when given the choice of walking or riding, she reluctantly gave in, reducing to the size of a collie.

"Oh, aren't you the cutest little thing," Monkey said as he hovered overhead.

"Just see how cute my claws are," Mistral snapped as she reared up and slashed at him.

Monkey had taken care to be just beyond her reach—much to her frustration.

"She won't always be that size," Räv said to the ape. "You sure like to live dangerously, don't you?"

Monkey polished his nails. "Boredom is the only thing that scares me."

Mistral, with her experience in flying, had assumed she would be handling the pi fang; but Mr. Hu insisted huffily that it was *his* responsibility to get them there. From the smile of anticipation on his master's face, Tom suspected the tiger simply wanted to fly himself.

The threadlike reins looked incredibly fragile in Mr. Hu's paws; they all held their breath as the cart wobbled along the ground and then lurched into the air, its wheels still spinning.

It was not the most elegant of takeoffs and the cart bobbed and rolled and once almost overturned. Fortunately, the threadlike reins were surprisingly strong as the tiger fought to right their vehicle.

Monkey had difficulty keeping up with the cart. "Tigers were never meant to fly, Hu."

Mr. Hu squinted at the ape. "Stop distracting me and let me concentrate."

From beneath them, they could hear Mistress Quick hiccoughing over and over, saying, "Oh dear, oh dear."

"Fly over the lake while you practice," shouted Master Thick from below. "That way if anyone falls out, they'll land in water."

It was touch and go whether they would make the lake; and in fact the cart's bottom grazed the tops of several trees. During the wild ride, Tom sank down in a corner, holding on to the phoenix's pouch with one hand and the cart's side with the other. He just hoped Master Yen had moved on with his castle.

Somehow they reached the lake, where Mistress Quick joined them in the air. Between hiccoughs, she managed to suggest that they let the pi fang do the flying; and when Mr. Hu gave in, they found themselves moving easily. But the tiger still insisted on holding the reins. "I," he explained stiffly, "am still the pilot of this cart."

With Mistress Quick's worried farewells ringing in their ears, the Guardian turned the cart toward the Imperfect Mountain once more. The yellow-and-black bird was soon lost to sight as they sped over the giant trees that covered the mountain slopes like a green carpet.

"I is hungry, Mama," the phoenix declared.

Tom undid the ribbon of multicolored fibers and unwrapped the cloth sack that Mistress Quick had given him. Somehow she had put a pattern of stars on the brown cotton. The phoenix ate all the seeds quickly. "That all?" he sniffed.

"They gave you as much as they could," Tom snarled. As he explained how hungry their hosts had been and what a sacrifice it was, the little bird started to tear up. "You can't order everyone around just because you're the king. You have to make sacrifices too."

"What is king then?" the phoenix asked with great seriousness.

"It's . . . it's like being a mama and a papa to all your subjects." Tom tried to explain and felt he was doing a poor job of it. "You have to take care of them just like we take care of you."

The little bird seemed to drink in every word and then thought quietly, until winds began to knock the cart this way and that and up and down as if they were lumbering along a bumpy road. The big wooden wheels revolved and rattled as if they were rolling on the ground instead of in the air. There were times when it was all the pi fang could do to keep upright and all Mistral could do to keep from throwing up.

"Oog," she moaned as her head weaved back and forth like a pendulum on her long neck.

Though Räv had wanted to stay on the ground, she

seemed to be enjoying herself. "This is like being on a roller coaster without rails."

Mistral lolled her head miserably on the side of the cart. "Double oog," she groaned.

Taking Tom's advice to heart, the phoenix skittered over the planks to the dragon. "Auntie all right?" the bird asked.

Mistral shut her eyes. "No, Auntie thinks she's going to be sick."

"Nonsense," Mr. Hu said over his shoulder. "How can a dragon get airsick?"

"Riding in a cart with a bumbling pilot is different than flying," Mistral said, struggling to get up. "Let me handle the reins."

A lurch of the cart made her plop back down and the miserable dragon laid her head upon the cart floor.

Mr. Hu remained where he was. "Sidney, see if you have any medicine for a weak stomach back there. And if not, then a plastic bag."

The rat had a tonic for everything, and as he ministered to the ill dragon, the phoenix scampered about the cart, unaffected by Mr. Hu's inexperienced piloting.

Finally, he skittered over to Tom. "I is still hungry, Mama!"

"Oog," Mistral said, closing her eyes. "How can you think of food at a time like this?"

Tom suggested that the others each take a turn giving

some crumbs to the little bird to cement the idea that they were all family. Even the sick dragon fed the phoenix. Sidney was still a little shy with him, trembling as he stretched out his paw and snatching it back as soon as the delicate beak had taken the morsel. "You know your uncle Sidney wouldn't hurt you, kiddo," he said with a nervous laugh.

"You're a growing boy, aren't you?" Räv asked as the phoenix hopped up and down, beak open, cheeping that he wanted more. "Say 'please.'"

"When have you ever said *please* in your life?" Tom teased her.

"I could ask the same," Räv shot back, and then said to the phoenix, "You don't want to grow up to be like me, do you, Junior?"

"Please, Papa," the phoenix begged the girl. He caught the crumb neatly in his beak, and swallowed it whole.

Räv tickled his belly. "And what do you say now?" she hinted.

"Yum," the phoenix said.

"No, you say . . ." Räv mouthed "thank you."

The sharp-eyed little bird understood and said, "Thank you, Papa." Then he opened his beak again. "More please, please, please."

The girl enjoyed her new role so much that she kept feeding him crumbs until the little bird's belly began to bulge.

"I think that's enough for now," Tom said. "He's like a guppy that will eat until it busts a gut."

"No," the phoenix snapped his beak. "I is king."

"No, that's enough," Tom growled.

When the little bird still did not get his way, he proceeded to throw a royal tantrum while Tom tried to quiet him down. Though he tried everything he could think of—from stern commands to begging—nothing stopped the phoenix.

"You're just tired and cranky, aren't you?" Räv said softly. Taking some flowers from Mistress Quick's bouquet, she nimbly wove a small wreath. "There. A crown for His Highness."

"Oo, pretty," the phoenix murmured, and then twitched in surprise when Räv placed it on his head.

Tom hadn't expected such a gentle skill from such a tough girl. He would have been less surprised if she had flapped her arms and flown into the sky.

"What?" she demanded as she felt his stare.

"Where did you learn to do that?"

Räv seemed embarrassed. "Not everything I picked up on the streets was bad."

Before the phoenix could shake off the crown, Räv said, "Look how handsome you are." Taking the stiletto from her other sleeve, the girl held it out so the phoenix could see his reflection upon the shiny blade.

"Handsome." The phoenix gave a decisive nod of his

head, which knocked his wreath askew. "And pretty!" He touched a wingtip to his wreath, glancing between Räv and Tom, and then urged, "Now one for Mama and Papa!"

"No way," Tom said.

The phoenix tipped his wreath even farther as he nodded vigorously. "Mama, Papa, Baby. We all have same."

Tom delicately adjusted the wreath with his fingers. "No thanks."

Mr. Hu looked over his shoulder. "Master Thomas, can't you see he wants you to be like him?"

Tom looked at Räv, expecting her to refuse, but she surprised him again by shrugging. "Anything to shut Junior up."

Having exhausted his few tricks as a parent, Tom surrendered. "I guess."

The girl's fingers skillfully wove the rest of the bouquet into wreaths, which she and Tom set upon their heads.

Tom glared at the others in warning, exposing his teeth as if they were fangs. "No jokes."

"I wouldn't think of it," Monkey said, hiding his smirk behind his paw as he added, "much." Sidney developed a sudden interest in a knothole in a plank and even the ill dragon's shoulders shook as if she were laughing silently.

"Would you like to rest and take your meal?" Mr. Hu called to the pi fang.

The bird flew with seeming ease. "You said His Highness's mission is urgent?"

"Yes. But we don't want to tax you."

The phoenix tugged at Mr. Hu's trousers. "Say 'please,' Grandpa."

Startled, the tiger looked down at the bird.

"Say 'please,'" the bird repeated.

"What kind of example are you setting, Hu?" Monkey teased. "Mind your manners, Grandpa."

With a glare at the ape, the Guardian mumbled, "Please rest if you wish."

"Since His Highness's errand is urgent, I won't let myself be tired," the pi fang declared.

They made another meal from some of Sidney's leftovers—with Monkey taking the pi fang's share and feeding him as he flapped along. And when they were finished eating, Mr. Hu resumed driving the cart, along with giving Tom his lessons. "I'll soon have you doing magic as well as any tiger," he insisted.

So, while Räv distracted the phoenix, the boy began learning the Lore again. Thinking about the dangers that might lie ahead of them, he tried his best to pay attention. But one thing had been bothering him and he finally asked, "How can Vatten cause the sky to fall?"

Mr. Hu raised his paw as if tracing a column. "So many lines of ch'i join at the mountain that they concentrate an enormous energy and weaken the laws of our physical universe."

"You make the sky sound like a roof," Tom objected.

"But it's air and water and other stuff."

Mr. Hu saw that his apprentice was still doubtful. "Let's approach this from another route. The Lore and human science agree that the physical universe is different forms of the same thing. The Lore tells us that the universe is composed of variations of the Way." He took one paw from the reins and patted the side of the cart. "On the other hand, human scientists would say that the cart's planks are nothing more than atoms like carbon and hydrogen and oxygen, which form molecules. These molecules, in turn, have joined together in even more complex combinations, which we call wood. Juggle those same atoms in different combinations and quantities and you would have your body."

Tom was trying hard to follow the tiger's reasoning. "So my body and the cart are the same thing?"

The tiger nodded. "Ultimately. But at an everyday level of experience, they are quite separate."

"Except at a special area like the mountain," Tom said.

"Exactly." Mr. Hu took the reins in both paws. "The mountain itself has its own function. The Lore calls the mountain a pillar of the sky, but in modern terms the mountain acts like a kind of machine that keeps reminding the molecules of the area to stay as they are. When Kung Kung broke the mountain, he damaged the 'machine' and the air molecules forgot they were gas and recombined into something solid. And then, like a roof

152

without supports, the solid sky began to break apart and fall. Worse, the 'forgetting' started to spread from that spot throughout the atmosphere."

"Until *she* patched the spot," Tom said. By *she*, he meant the mysterious Empress Nü Kua whose name he didn't dare mention.

"With the help of the seal, the mountain can carry out its original purpose despite the damage," Mr. Hu explained.

Then the tiger launched into a lecture on the points where quantum mechanics resembled magic until Tom's head swam; he was glad when his master returned to the ins and outs of cold spells.

Deep in the evening, the moon hung like a huge silvery disk; its soft glow transformed the streams to gleaming mercury and silvered the forest canopy. The phoenix, however, had eyes only for the stars.

"It's nice to see things through the eyes of a child," Mr. Hu observed.

"Pretty, Mama. But they is too small," the phoenix murmured.

It took Tom a moment to figure out the phoenix was comparing them to the crystal star in the Chinatown shop. "They look that way," he agreed, "because we're far away. But if you got up close, they'd be a lot bigger than that crystal." He hadn't realized the little bird treasured the memory so much, and he was sorry he hadn't been able to buy the crystal for him.

The chick lay on Tom's lap and continued to stare up at the stars. Eventually, they both fell asleep there. Tom did not wake again until dawn, when the cart rocked as they landed. Mr. Hu informed them the pi fang needed to rest.

Giant trees with huge moss-covered roots grew all around, with brush and smaller trees clustering around, forming green walls all around the clearing.

Raised in San Francisco, Tom would have found the woods a more intimidating place if Mr. Hu and his friends had not been there. A glance at Räv told him that the forest was having the same effect on her, for she had also lived all her life in a city.

Down the slope, through the pine trees, Tom glimpsed the valley where the forest gave way to lush meadows. He felt as if he were sitting on the rim of a giant green bowl and would much rather be in the center, because it would be in the open. But who knew what other monsters and brigands might be traveling there?

Mr. Hu was immediately at home in the dark, dense forest. His eyes roved around and he continually sniffed the air, as much for his own pleasure as out of caution. Tom didn't have enough tiger's blood to make him share the Guardian's love of the woods.

Tom had thought the tiger would take a nap along with the pi fang, but he said, "We need to supplement

Sidney's stores." And he loped off before anyone could say anything. Though the excuse was reasonable, it was clear the tiger simply wanted to roam in the forest.

To Tom's surprise, Räv sprang to her feet and took from the cart some of the water jars Mistress Quick had given them. "Yeah, and I'll refill these. I thought we passed over a stream." But she also took along an empty basket.

Mistral grew back to her regular size. "Monkey, go with her—just in case there are more 'rowdies' in the neighborhood. I'll guard the children and the phoenix."

"I can take care of myself," Räv said, disappearing into the forest.

Mistral said nothing, merely nodded her head at Monkey, who transformed some of his tail hairs into little apes and sent them scampering after the girl.

Tom told himself that Räv had proved her loyalty many times by now—but before she had been the rebel's ambassador, she had served Vatten well as a spy. He couldn't help wondering if she might switch sides again and scolded himself for entertaining such suspicions.

The little apes returned before the girl or Mr. Hu, and when they whispered in Monkey's ear, he gave a chuckle.

Räv looked almost ashamed when she came back. Putting the refilled jars into the cart, she sat down on a log with the basket on her lap.

"Not pretty," the phoenix said, regarding his wilted wreath.

155

"I'll make you a new one," the girl promised, and from the basket she took a bunch of freshly picked flowers.

"Thank you, Papa," the bird remembered to say.

"Sometime, you and I are going to have a long talk, Junior," Räv said, but she was smiling when she set the wreath upon his head.

"You went off to get flowers?" Tom asked.

Räv hunched her shoulders. "What's wrong with that?"

"It's just very . . . kind," Tom said, and couldn't help grinning.

"It's not like I'm turning soft or anything," Räv said as she nimbly wove a new wreath.

When Mr. Hu returned with his forage, they woke the pi fang and made a meager meal—even Mistral was willing to eat now that she was on the ground again, which left the rest of them almost as hungry as when they began. But the phoenix was happy. "Picnic," he said, spreading his wings to include the group, "like in book."

For five days they followed the same routine, and every day Räv went to pick flowers for the phoenix as if she were beginning to enjoy being his father.

On the sixth day, they reached the pass. It slashed through the mountains like a sword cut and the canyon walls were sheer and smooth—they looked like translucent glass that had been colored with shades of gray and black, then striped with red and brown. The winds became even trickier here, as if they were slipping on the slick canyon sides; and it was all Mr. Hu could do to keep the cart from slamming against the pass.

He strained and tugged at the reins, hissing to himself, his face creased in worry. Several times Monkey had to help steady the cart; and poor Mistral, who had been sick for each day of the flight, even used Sidney's airsick bag.

As the pi fang fought to keep them upright, they finally reached the mouth of the pass. Before them swept a wasteland the color of dried blood. At a distance, it reminded Tom of a piece of ugly fabric that had been draped carelessly over the landscape, lying in folds or heaped in strange mounds.

The cart steadied as they left the mountains and the pi fang flew with slow, steady beats of its wings. The heat rose from the ground, wrapping itself around them like warm, invisible towels; and Tom began to feel sorry for his friends with fur or scales, not to mention Mr. Hu, who wore a suit over his fur.

Holding the reins in one paw, Mr. Hu slipped his handkerchief from his pocket to mop his face. "The Lore says that this was once a green paradise."

As they flew ahead, Tom found it hard to believe, for the arid land beneath them was shattered into hill-size lumps and gashed for mile after mile with dry gullies, as if giant monsters had torn and slashed it in a mad fury.

There wasn't a sign of life and the air felt hot and dead.

Tom was glad they were flying, rather than trying to make the trek on foot. "Did the war against Kung Kung do all this damage?"

Mr. Hu jerked his head toward a hill with a rounded dome and sharp, triangular sides. "What do you think? That's a fossilized skull of one of his followers."

"But that's huge!" Tom said.

"Kung Kung had many titanic monsters. That's why it cost so many lives to defeat him," Mr. Hu replied. "The Lore says it did not feel like a victory."

"And this war against Vatten could cost even more," Mistral added grimly. Now that the cart was traveling smoothly, she had recovered a bit.

As hot as the wasteland was in the daytime, it turned freezing at night and they lay huddled together for warmth. Tom cradled the phoenix carefully in his arms. It would have been hard to believe that the small, fragile bird had such power had he not seen it with his own eyes.

Fortunately for everyone's peace of mind, Räv had stockpiled flowers, which she made into a wreath for the phoenix, and Mr. Hu cast a spell to keep them fresh.

It was the next afternoon that they sighted the first of Vatten's monsters. Monkey swooped in and landed in the cart almost on top of Mistral.

"Oof, I'm not a carpet," she complained, shoving him away.

"No, a carpet's better behaved," the ape said. "We've got company, Hu."

Mr. Hu looked all around. "I don't see anything."

"The sides of that gully are hiding them right now," Monkey said, pointing below where the land folded upon itself like clay. "But I saw several dozen p'ao. They should be marching into sight about . . . now."

Curious, Tom started to lean over, but Mistral caught his robe. "Don't let them see you. If all they see is the pi fang and the cart, they'll think there's just chu huai inside."

Peeking over the side, Tom saw the first p'ao appear in the open. From this high up, it looked like a goat, but he had encountered them in an ambush on the roof of Mr. Hu's store, so he knew they had fangs as sharp as the Guardian's.

More p'ao followed their leader and several rose on their hind legs to raise their front ones. It might have been a greeting, but it also might have been because their eyes were not in their heads but just behind their forelegs.

Mr. Hu surveyed the broken land with all of its many deep fissures snaking their way toward the horizon. "You could hide a whole army here and never see them."

"We'll have to keep a sharp watch when we rest," Mistral advised.

"Well, what hides them can hide us," Monkey said.

"I was going to start traveling more at night anyway,"

Mr. Hu said, "when it's cooler."

At midday, during the hottest hours, they rested in deep canyons; and while Tom welcomed what relief the canyon shadows gave, he nonetheless felt trapped, for the steep sides shut out all but a winding ribbon of blue sky.

He was grateful when they could resume their journey in the twilight just before sunset. In the clear desert air, the stars and moon shone brighter and appeared nearer, with points so sharp Tom felt like ducking. Meanwhile, the phoenix sat upon his lap, gazing raptly at the stars.

Tom, his tiger eyes glowing amber in the dark, sighted the next monsters. They had emerged from one canyon, intent upon reaching another, and their tracks stood out like dotted lines in the moonlight. Then he saw the creatures themselves.

Though they had bodies like humans', they had heads like tigers', and instead of hands they had tentacles that wriggled like snakes; and when they opened their mouths, more tentacles spread outward. They moved with jerky motions like insects. Just looking at them made Tom's skin crawl.

"*Chiang ling,*" Räv said next to him. "They'll kill for the sake of killing."

"Let's hope Master Yen spoke the truth about the mountain being guarded," Mr. Hu said.

They spotted more monsters, but at Mr. Hu's urging, the pi fang flew so high they were mere specks.

* * *

As Räv made the customary wreath on the seventh day, she measured the phoenix with her eyes. "You know, it's taking more flowers to make a wreath for you. If I didn't know any better, I'd say you were getting bigger by the minute."

Tom was so used to the phoenix that he had not really thought about it, but now that Räv mentioned it, the bird's legs and neck did seem to be longer, and his feathers seemed to be less like down and more like fine wires.

Mr. Hu glanced at the phoenix critically. "Yes, he does seem to be maturing exceptionally fast. And he's been speaking better. It may be some aftereffect of the magic the dragons used to hatch him."

They reached the Imperfect Mountain without further incident a little after dawn that day. The mountain soared so high above the wasteland that it truly seemed like a pillar, and it was hard to believe that anyone could reach its peak, but Mr. Hu pointed to the flat top and said the tip had been lopped off by Kung Kung.

While Mr. Hu had the pi fang circle, he indicated the deep gashes in the steep yellow sides, where red rock was exposed like raw wounds. "That's more of Kung Kung's handiwork."

The tingling at the back of Tom's neck began to grow steadily until he felt as if dozens of little electric worms were dancing there. "Even if the top's been chopped off, there's a lot of ch'i here," he said.

"It's not just ch'i that's gathered here." Monkey frowned and pointed at the ground below them.

The rising sun glinted blood red from the translucent wings of a trio of suan-yü.

With the end of the flight in sight, Mistral recovered enough to peer over the side. "Is that all the garrison there is?"

The suan-yü lurched into the air, climbing toward them rapidly with their beating wings now a blur.

The sharp-eyed tiger picked out the rider on the back of one of the mechanical creatures. "I see Master Yen too."

Monkey landed on the side of the cart in a show of casualness, but his paw was poised to grab the needle tucked behind his ear. "He's come to take us back to his palace."

Mistral grunted. "Won't he be surprised when Vatten and his army come to visit."

Monkey slipped the needle out, and in the wink of an eye it grew into a staff that he twirled easily in his paw. "Then it's up to us to save the day yet again."

CHAPTER TWELVE

The cart rocked up and down and sideways in the downdraft from the suan-yü's wings, which beat with loud clicks like sticks drawn over a picket fence. Their long, thin bodies were coiled like whips and their jaws were open, revealing sharp wooden fangs. They darted with the agility of scaled hummingbirds as they gradually herded the cart downward. Tom's neck ached as he twisted to keep all the threats in sight.

Master Yen didn't seem upset by the zigging and zagging of his mount. "Everyone else is searching all over for you, but I thought you'd head here," he said with immense smugness. There was a deep bruise around one eye, a memento of Räv's ruse at the party.

The pi fang had no choice but to guide the cart down. "Three guards? Three?" Mr. Hu demanded. "I thought there'd at least be some of the younger heroes here. Did you really think three robots were enough to guard the mountain?"

"Actually, it was only a pair of guards. The third brought me from the palace. Thanks to you, I had only this servant left." Master Yen smiled thinly as he slipped a handful of magical charms from his sleeve. "But it's time for just deserts." He fanned the paper slips like cards, ready to fling them at the Guardian. "You won't find my palace nearly as luxurious when I bring you back. Perhaps some of your underlings can even help with the repairs."

Tom clutched the phoenix protectively as the pi fang set down the cart with a jarring bump; gradually it rolled to a stop. Now that they were no longer in motion, the hot, still air felt as heavy as a blanket.

Mr. Hu inclined his head to speak to Master Yen, who continued to circle their heads. "I'm afraid we'll have to decline your hospitality. Vatten's army is headed here." And the tiger told him about their encounter with the chu huai and what they had seen during their flight.

Mistral had taken care to grow to her usual intimidating length as soon as she had stepped onto the ground. "Vatten must have hidden until he recovered, and now he's coming to have his vengeance just as we warned you."

As eager as Master Yen was to take his prizes to his palace, he could not ignore the threat and dispatched two of his suan-yü to scout out the wastelands.

But word was brought by the dragons instead, barely an hour after his servants had left.

The Dragon King loomed over them like a large emerald-and-gold cloud. Above him were nine more dragons, with Tench as their leader. "The lands are crawling with Vatten's scum," he announced distastefully as he swept a paw to indicate the broken land. "When we saw where they were heading, I, ahem, realized we may have misjudged the danger. So we came here as fast as we could."

The ground shook repeatedly as the weary king and each of his ten guards landed.

"Just how many monsters did you see?" Mr. Hu asked.

"Several dozen," the Dragon King said. His armor was dented and the steel tip of one claw was broken off. "However, some of them will not be keeping their appointment."

Master Yen peered at the horizon. "Then we must get the Guardian to safety before we prepare the defense."

"And for every one His Majesty saw, there are probably ten more. With all your strength and skill"—the tiger nodded first at the Dragon King and then at Master Yen—"you will not be able to counter such numbers. And what good will it do to hide when Vatten destroys the mountain?"

"But what if he captures the phoenix here?" Master Yen argued.

Between taking care of the phoenix and his lessons in

the Lore, Tom had been giving a lot of thought to this matter during their long journey. "It . . . it won't do him any good." He was so frightened that his voice came out as a whisper, but it grew louder as he went on. He held the little bird up in front of his face. "You're never to obey Vatten. You're only to obey me or Grandpa."

"Yes, Mama." The phoenix nodded.

Räv understood immediately and her quick-witted mind leaped one step ahead. "No matter what someone might do to them or us," she added.

The phoenix looked startled but nodded again. "Yes, Papa."

"Well done, Master Thomas and Mistress Räv!" the Guardian declared. "You're maturing as fast as your child."

Master Yen took a deep breath and let it out. "Then it's either the world or nothing now."

"Are you sure you can't open a gate to summon help?" Mistral appealed to Master Yen.

Master Yen shook his head. "The powers of this place make it impossible. I had to fly here myself. Reinforcements will need to come to us the old-fashioned way—by wing, paw, or foot."

Mr. Hu turned to the Dragon King. "The dragons have performed many heroic deeds for the sake of the world, but are they noble enough to sacrifice their pride? Will

166

you find and bring back help?"

The Dragon King reared back angrily, and it was quite an awesome sight to see the brilliant eyes glaring down at them from so high. "So we should let them ride upon our backs as if we were . . . ponies?"

"I would not ask if there wasn't a need," Mr. Hu said.

Slowly the proud head dipped. "Let no one say we dragons weren't willing to give everything for the sake of the world. Even *I* will do as you ask, Guardian, and carry as many riders as I can."

Tom was standing by Mistral when the dragons left. She moved her paws restlessly as if she wished she were going with them. Even though her own kind had lied and mistreated her, the same blood still flowed through her veins.

The Dragon King spread his great wings like a scaled wall and then brought them down with such force that he raised a small dust storm. Upward he soared, and one by one his warriors joined him as he circled high overhead. Despite the distance, their mighty wings created a wind below. And then, like arrows shot from bows, the dragons darted in all directions on their desperate mission.

"He might be a lying, cheating worm," Mistral said grudgingly, "but he's no coward."

While they waited, Master Yen paced back and forth, scanning the skies, and Mr. Hu took to prowling with him.

The tiger's restlessness triggered the same reaction in Tom, and he found himself wanting to stalk about with the Guardian, but Räv stopped him. "You can't take Junior out into the sun, even in a pouch," she scolded. Tom reluctantly retreated into the shade of the boulder where they were sitting, but he could not keep his feet from fidgeting.

The only thing he could do while waiting was listen to the spring bubbling up in a stone pond at the foot of the mountain. Towering above the pond was a giant figure carved upon the rocks of the spring. It was so worn by the elements that Tom could barely make out that it appeared to be a human woman from the waist up and a snake from the waist down. The words above her head were even more weathered, and in an archaic script, but Tom could just make them out—Gift of the Empress. He knew there could be only one empress to whom that referred and that was Nü Kua.

Mr. Hu was the first to spot the dark cloud and he sniffed the air. "We've reinforcements of a sort."

When the cloud drew nearer, Tom could see that they were birds, hundreds of them, of every size and color, and as they landed, he saw that a number of them bore a resemblance to Mistress Quick. But there was a tall, angular crane as well and even a majestic falcon, settling among the birds that were usually its prey. Tom supposed there was some temporary truce—though the other birds still kept a wary distance from the hunter.

Mistress Quick was indeed part of the group, and she hovered in the air until Tom held up his arm as a perch where she could alight.

"Oh, thank Heavens we found you," Mistress Quick puffed. "I was so worried, Master Thick suggested I come here to take care of His Highness."

"And the rest of your flock?" Tom asked.

"I told a few friends and kin where I was going and . . . well . . . word spread," the bird confessed. "Everyone wanted to meet His Highness."

"Hungry," the phoenix said.

His voice had an electric effect upon the other birds, who rose into the air, twittering and cawing excitedly.

Mistress Quick was pleased. "We thought a growing chick like yourself might be a bit peckish, so we brought gifts for you." Opening her claw, she dropped several seeds upon the ground. "Come, pay homage to your king."

Then, one by one, each bird brought its offering. Most of them were more seeds—except the falcon, who had brought a dead rabbit. Soon the pile of food rose up to Tom's ankles. Knowing how Vatten's monsters had stripped the land of food, he knew this was another precious sacrifice.

"Eat, eat," the birds urged with chirps and squawks.

The phoenix gazed at his subjects instead. "They is so thin."

"Times have been hard for them," Tom said gently.

The phoenix spread his wings like twin flames. "We share. We is family. You eat. I is your king." The phoenix glanced at Tom. "No," the fast-maturing bird corrected himself, "I is your mama and papa."

The words sent his subjects wheeling back into the air like a bright, multicolored banner that rippled and flapped in the wind. The birds' open joy lifted all their spirits, and Tom felt his hopes rise as high as the flock.

"No king had a better flag," Mr. Hu murmured.

"I do good, Mama?" the phoenix whispered.

Tom felt a strange thrill, realizing the little bird had tried to act on what his mother had taught him. "Yes," he said with a lump in his throat, "you did good."

Suddenly the falcon broke from the others and hovered. "Someone's coming," he called.

And the flock dissolved, darting this way and that in confusion. The defenders prepared themselves, crouching anxiously until Mr. Hu straightened in relief and told them it was K'ua Fu.

Tired and dusty, the tattooed warrior trudged toward them. "Ah, I see I'm not too late," he said. "I met a few members of Vatten's former army intent upon reaching the mountain, so I figured I'd better come too." He headed past them to the stone pond.

The tattoos on the back of K'ua Fu's hands and head began to glow. Tom jumped as nests of serpents, the color of sulfur, came alive and wriggled out from behind K'ua Fu's ears and the backs of his hands. They began to hiss, as if sensing their master's thirst.

The spectacle frightened the birds, who twittered in alarm. Mistress Quick fluttered protectively before the phoenix.

K'ua Fu did not seem to notice the effect he was having. He threw himself upon the rocks and thrust both his head and hands into the water, which bubbled as he and his serpents drank.

"Those snakes always give me such a headache when they wriggle," Monkey muttered, rubbing his eyes. "Have you got any aspirin, Sidney?"

"Sorry," the rat said. "I used them up on the ride."

Even Master Yen had turned pale at the spectacle. Mr. Hu was the only one who acted as if K'ua Fu's horde of snakes was as harmless as worms. "Steady, Master Thomas," he murmured to his apprentice. "This is nothing. If you want to see something truly upsetting, you should see him and his pets eat dinner."

Having satisfied his thirst and that of his pets, K'ua Fu got to his knees and bowed his head to the carving of the Empress. The sight of her likeness seemed to calm his serpents as they settled back into his head and hands.

Mistress Quick sat on Tom's shoulder and stared uneasily at K'ua Fu. "It's really not for me to say, Your Highness, but you do have the most unusual friends."

Mr. Hu bowed. "Mistress Quick, will you do another service to your king?"

"Gladly," the bird said.

"Will you and your companions scout about the wasteland and tell us who's coming?"

"Please," the phoenix reminded him.

Mr. Hu dipped his head in acknowledgement. "Yes, please."

"Of course," she said, fluttering into the air and soaring up to the others still flying overhead. "His Highness has a mission for us."

She disappeared within the flock for a moment and then the cloud seemed to burst as they dispersed in all directions—hundreds of feathered spies whom no one would suspect. Mistress Quick, however, returned to the phoenix, resting on Tom's shoulder when she was not seeing to her king's needs or hovering to fan him with her wings.

During the rest of the day, most of the news that Master Yen's servants and their feathered scouts brought back was grim. From the descriptions the birds gave, Mr. Hu recognized different types of Vatten's monsters and their numbers. Räv kept a tally, scraping it in the dirt. The count had reached four hundred and ninety-three before they heard some good news again.

Ch'ih Yu and his five brothers were marching now to their aid. Soon they saw a cloud of dust raised by their feet, and the bronze-headed warrior strode straight to the tiger. Both his head and shield had numerous dents and he was cut and bruised.

"No gloating, Guardian. I admit you were right." He wiped some of the dust from his metal head. "Even before I received Master Yen's message, we had met monsters heading here and I knew we must come."

Mr. Hu used his handkerchief to wipe the sweat and dust from his fur. "I take no pleasure in being correct."

By late afternoon, the monster count had reached more than one thousand. More help arrived but it was pitifully small. Lady Torka flew in with seven other warriors from the east, having received word from one of the birds.

The raven-winged Dark Lady arrived shortly after from the west, flying with three warriors. Everyone immediately deferred to these two experts to plan the defense of the mountain.

They were both dismayed when they were shown the tally of Vatten's monsters scratched into the dirt.

Lady Torka brushed her bone fan angrily across it. "We have forces all around the world. If only we had the time to muster them, we could destroy Vatten once and for all."

The Dark Lady took off her feathered helmet to reveal

short, dark hair clinging to her damp head. "Vatten knows that we could crush him if he delays, so he won't allow our force to grow any larger. Battles are won not by the size of an army but by who has the greatest numbers in the right spot." She smiled ruefully at Mr. Hu. "It might have been otherwise if we had heeded the Guardian's warning in the first place."

"Oh, why didn't we?" Lady Torka bowed apologetically first to Mr. Hu and then to Räv. "But we were foolish, and believed only what we wanted to believe. Nor could we cast aside ancient suspicions of one another. Now the odds are against us. It seems we have seriously underestimated Vatten, and overestimated ourselves."

The Dark Lady surveyed the desolate land around the broken mountain. "We won't again."

"One way or another," Lady Torka said with a savage smile. "We should have listened to the Guardian and continued to trust one another."

Ch'ih Yu thumped the end of his spear against the ground. "We've saved the world before. Or are you getting old, Dark Lady? Are those gray hairs I spy?"

The Dark Lady held her helmet against her side. "They are no more gray than yours."

"And yet despite all we've done, who remembers us now?" Master Yen demanded, glancing meaningfully at Tom. "The Guardian's own apprentice didn't recognize me when we first met. And when I walked around Chinatown, I saw no altars or statues in our honor. The children of this world have forgotten us."

"Are you suggesting that we have outlived our usefulness?" The Dark Lady fluttered her wings like an angry cloud.

Master Yen folded his arms. "How can living legends really be legends if no one recalls them?"

Ch'ih Yu rubbed his forehead with a squeaking sound. "Bah, this is a time for strategy, not philosophy."

"I bow to your common sense." The Dark Lady laughed as she sat, using her helmet as a stool.

They were still discussing their plans when the sun began to set. It was then that the dragons appeared from the darkening lands to the east, and upon their backs they brought Lord Trumma, Lord Harnal, and their troops.

The Dragon King was no longer the glorious-looking ruler who had greeted Mr. Hu within his winter palace. He could barely fly because of the savage tears in his left wing, and his scaled body was gashed and scarred all over. He tried to land elegantly but his injured wing wouldn't let him, and he crashed heavily on one side, throwing his riders off.

He lay exhausted for a moment while Lord Trumma picked himself up awkwardly saying, "Rest, friend."

"No, I must tell the news myself," the Dragon King

insisted. His warriors made to help him up, but he shook them off, lurching upright on his own to stand shakily upon his legs. Lord Trumma stayed near to help him, though it was doubtful even his great strength could support a dragon.

"Vatten's monsters have rendezvoused at a shining column of mist," reported the Dragon King, licking cracked lips. "We encountered them on our way here but fought clear."

The Dark Lady rose quickly, filled her helmet from the pool, and carried it to the king. "He is probably hiding inside that column, since water is one of his elements and gives him extra power."

The Dragon King gratefully took the helmet and gulped from it like a cup. "I would wager that as well. Both the column and the monsters are advancing in haste. I have never seen such determination. The creatures drive on though they have little water and even less food. They will be here on the morrow."

Lady Torka spun around to appeal to Mr. Hu. "Guardian, the odds are so great against us. Won't you use the phoenix to tame our enemies?"

The little bird peered around curiously as all eyes turned toward him. "Mama says not to hurt anyone," he said firmly.

"The phoenix is barely hatched and yet he's so much wiser than you," Mr. Hu said, sweeping a paw to indicate them all. "Yes, I could ask him to tame our enemies and we would win a great victory. But we would lose the real war against our own greed and ambition."

The Dragon King whipped his head back and forth impatiently and stomped a paw so hard on the ground that it started small avalanches of pebbles and sent some roosting birds squawking into the air. "Yes, yes, we know the history of the Guardians, but the choice is clear: If you don't use the phoenix, Vatten will. He'll take over the world, now that you've delivered the bird into his hand."

Master Yen's shoulders sagged resignedly. "The phoenix has been commanded never to obey Vatten."

"So the Guardian has doomed the world"—Ch'ih Yu spat contemptuously—"just so he can save his precious honor."

"You've taken away our greatest weapon," Lord Harnal squealed. He had clearly been depending upon the phoenix as the last resort, as had several of the others, judging from the disappointment and frustration on their faces.

The Guardian thrust his head forward and growled from deep in his throat, "If I ever began to use the phoenix, how long would it be before you became my slave?" He strode around the circle of leaders, lashing his tail back and forth. "I am not so arrogant as to think I am immune to power once I taste it. It would only be a matter of time before I gave in to the next temptation and began to 'correct' all the things that I thought wrong. And then I would become a greater threat than Vatten. And how long would it be before each of you decided you could use the phoenix more wisely than me and came to take him for yourself?"

As the tiger gazed at each of the council in turn, several dropped their eyes guiltily as if they had been thinking just the same thing; but only the Dragon King dared to speak up. "Perhaps one of us should take the phoenix now." His eyes narrowed to dangerous slits. "Someone who is not afraid to let him use his power."

The tiger's ears flattened and his claws extended silently from his paws. "You would not find it easy. And wouldn't Vatten love us to start brawling among ourselves right now?"

The Dark Lady picked up her helmet, brushing off the dust. "Enough! The Guardian is right. We must not use the phoenix. We can only fight as we have always fought—with honor."

Lord Trumma had hopped over to the pool to wet his scarf. "Then we'll have to fight with the few we have."

The Dark Lady set the helmet back upon her head. "But with the greater glory when we win."

From her perch upon Tom's shoulder, Mistress Quick rose to all six inches of her height. "We will defend His Highness too. Don't forget his subjects."

Lord Trumma tittered as he flicked his wet scarf

toward her. "What can you feather dusters do against monsters?"

The falcon swooped down, forcing Lord Trumma to duck, then gyred upward for another dive. "Shall we see who is the better warrior?"

Lord Trumma jabbed his horns after the falcon. "By all means."

Spreading her wings, the Dark Lady flew over the rocks to the pool and seized one of his horns. He grunted angrily and the sinews stood out upon his great neck, but the lady forced his head down. "What Lord Trumma means is that His Highness's subjects have done more than enough," she called up diplomatically to the falcon. "You should leave now."

The falcon banked and landed by Tom's feet. "I stay with His Highness."

"And so do I," Mistress Quick chirped.

"And I," a voice cheeped as a tiny bird settled down next to the falcon.

When the birds all joined in a chorus, the Dark Lady released Lord Trumma and smiled at them. "Then, since you are the royal guard, will you take your place with His Highness and the Guardian up there?" She pointed to a ledge farther up the slope and then turned to Lady Torka. "Do you concur, Lady Torka?"

Lady Torka tapped her closed fan against a paw. "An army, like a body, should have only one head. I defer to you. It's said you have taught many great warriors and generals."

"But none was as skilled as you in battle," the Dark Lady said tactfully. "May I count on you for advice?"

"Of course. And if I may make a suggestion, then?" Lady Torka wriggled her fan toward the birds. "Perhaps you might have one more mission for the phoenix's guards. I see an owl among them. Send him out to keep an eye on Vatten's advance."

Other nocturnal birds volunteered as well, and after they had been sent off, the Dark Lady began to assign positions to the sparse defenders.

Lord Harnal's quilled pigs would take the left flank and Ch'ih Yu the right. Lord Trumma would anchor the center with K'ua Fu while Lady Torka would guard the sky. The Dark Lady, the dragons, and Master Yen would act as the reserves for the coming battle.

The Dark Lady wheeled about. "And now, Monkey, I witnessed your . . . um . . . special talents at Master Yen's palace. Can you sow discord among our enemies as well as among your friends?"

In appreciation of the lady's strategy, Lord Harnal gave a shake that rattled his quills and added: "Some of the factions hate one another almost as much as they hate us."

Monkey rubbed his paws together, relishing the challenge. "So I'll have my little apes whisper in ears and hearing holes, spreading all sorts of rumors and insults."

Laying down his staff, he began to yank out hairs from his tail with both paws, until his head was hidden in a cloud of gnat-size monkeys. The others could hear him whispering instructions from within, but they could not make out the actual words. The next instant, the little apes scattered, flitting away to reveal a smug-looking Monkey.

Puffing out his chest, he almost skipped about, so impressed was he with his cleverness. "And when the time is ripe, I, the Great Sage Equal to Heaven and Master of Seventy-Two Transformations, will harvest the crop my little apes have sown." Pivoting, he gave a low bow. "Dark Lady, be ready to strike when the moment is right."

Everyone but Master Yen found it hard not to smile, and the Dark Lady clasped her hands behind her back in amusement. "And what will be the sign?"

"You'll know when you see it." Springing confidently into the air, he somersaulted away, whipping over the wasteland in a blur.

The Dragon King winced as he tried to shift his weight to face Mistral. "I know there is no love lost between us, but will you put aside your differences with me today? I ask not for myself but for your race. We have need of your fresh strength."

Mistral sprang from the ground, lithe as a panther. "My race?" she asked sharply. "Are you forgetting you exiled me again?"

Mr. Hu cleared his throat. "Can't you put aside your

feud temporarily? There'll be enough fighting for all of us against Vatten."

Nodding grudgingly, Mistral turned to the king. "I cannot fly, so I will keep pace on the ground instead of in the air."

"On paw or wing, you're a great warrior," the Dragon King said.

Mistral gritted her fangs. "Then I'll join you for this day. But afterward, we'll have to settle matters between us."

"You're very confident we'll live to see another day." The Dragon King laughed grimly.

Mistral twisted her head upon her long, elegant neck and nudged Tom. "Keep yourself and the phoenix safe." And then, as proudly as though she were still a duchess, she strode over the stones to join the dragons as they took up their positions.

The meal the defenders ate next was a far cry from the feast in the Sky Palace, and the rocky slope far less luxurious than Master Yen's home. And yet high upon the ledge, the phoenix sat contentedly in Tom's lap while Räv fed him some of the crumbs from the last of Sidney's cakes. It was now a bit stale, and the phoenix began to cough, so the girl solicitously brought him water with a cup borrowed from Sidney.

Full at last, the phoenix settled back comfortably against Tom's stomach, watching the rainbow-colored flock gather on the rocks as they finished the offerings that they had brought him. "This is real picnic."

The sky blazed with reds and oranges that quickly gave way to purples and then an ebony blackness. The stars sparkled and the crescent moon smiled, silvering the wings of the birds.

The phoenix gazed lovingly up at Tom and then at his followers and finally up at the heavens.

"I is . . . no, I *am* happy," the phoenix announced as he stood up, his eyes shining. "I feel full of stars."

Wetting a fingertip, Tom slicked down an unruly tuft of feathers on the chick's head. "That's good."

"I want everyone to feel this way." Throwing back his head, the phoenix gazed at the stars and began to sing. Though his young voice lacked volume, it carried, trilling higher and higher and then dipping as if it were itself a bird in flight. Tom felt his own heart soaring with the song as if they would not stop rising until they reached the stars. And all doubts disappeared from his heart. Anything seemed possible, even beating Vatten and all his monsters.

Wherever they stood or sat, the warriors turned as one to gaze at the little bird, and the gruff Lord Harnal was so moved by the phoenix's song that he began to cry.

Tom thought he had never felt more hopeful or happier than he did at that moment, and the wonder of it lingered with him and the others long after the little bird had finished and retired into his pouch to sleep.

"And this too is the phoenix's power," Mr. Hu murmured

with an awed expression on his face.

Then the tiger drew the children down to pillow their heads against him. And Tom heard the deep rumbling sound and felt the vibrations against his cheek as the tiger began to purr.

CHAPTER THIRTEEN

The Hsing-t'ien
They once rebelled against Heaven and were punished. Now their eyes are in their chests and their mouths are where their belly buttons used to be. They like to dance holding shields and battle-axes.

The Fei
Their white heads are shaped like an ox's but with only a single eye and their tails are like snakes. Wherever they tread, the grass dies and rivers disappear. They are an omen of plague.

—Shan Hai Ching

The next morning Tom woke to the sound of distant thunder—which was odd because the sky was clear. Mr. Hu, looking very somber, told them it was the sound of Vatten's army. Hour after hour the noise increased until it seemed as if the earth had become a gigantic drum being struck by a horde of hooves, paws, and clawed feet.

The marching monsters stirred up a cloud of dust that slowly expanded from a fringe on the horizon until it covered the plain before the mountain. When they finally halted and the dust had settled, Tom saw creatures straight out of his

185

nightmares. Row after row of monsters had mustered at their master's command; standing in even ranks, they squinted against the sun in their eyes. Everywhere, bright blue banners flew, emblazoned with purple serpentine 9's.

Behind the monsters writhed a bloodred cloud twisting upward like some giant worm gnawing into the belly of the sky. Tom felt the tingling at the base of his neck.

Mr. Hu gazed at the misty column. Crouching instinctively, his muscles strained as if it was all he could do to keep his body from leaping to the attack. "Vatten," he growled. His tail began to whip back and forth.

Räv stroked the head of the phoenix, who peered anxiously from his pouch. "You could make a victory so easy," she said to Mr. Hu and Tom.

"What makes a Guardian is neither intellect nor magic nor martial skills," the tiger said, making an effort to straighten his tie despite the extreme conditions. "It's character. It's the ability to do the correct thing no matter the cost."

Annoyed, Räv waved her club. "How can you fuss with your clothes at a time like this?"

"It is precisely because it is a time like this. It reminds me I am not a wild beast but a civilized creature who must fight with a clear head. I'll need every advantage I have against Vatten, so whatever I do, I must keep hold of my temper." He smiled down at his apprentice, who was hastily dusting off the tiger's vest. "Your grandmother used to say that the mind is the deadliest weapon of all."

186

Tom looked up. "She did?"

Mr. Hu pulled at his cuffs. "She reminded me often when she was trying to teach me to be calm and collected." He touched his skull. "Usually before her knuckle rapped me on the forehead."

"Great-grandma hurt you?" the phoenix asked.

"They were merely love taps." The tiger smiled, lightly tapping his own brow in illustration.

The red cloud began to glow brighter until the army seemed washed by a sea of blood. And a thousand throats began to howl and scream, rising in volume until the phoenix covered his ears with his wingtips.

Wheeling and screeching overhead were grotesque creatures with furred bodies like apes and the heads of owls but with human noses and mouths. In their paws they held wicked-looking machetes. The Alliance had encountered these creatures before.

"Ugh, jen-mien hsiao." The rat shuddered. "I was hoping we'd seen the last of those guys." Hurriedly he began to sharpen his hatchet blade upon a stone.

Lady Torka clinked her metal-edged wings together confidently. "There is no way they can match me, so that gives at least one advantage."

"That is true of any monster out there on the ground as well," K'ua Fu said as his tattoos began to flicker to life. "But collectively there are more than enough monsters to sweep us away."

BATTLE ORDER

VATTEN

Front Line

Monsters	Hsing-t'ien	Fei

2nd Line

Monsters	Chiang Ling	Chu Huai

Reserve

Monsters	Monsters	Monsters
	Vatten	

ALLIANCE

Front Line
Lord Harnal   Lord Trumma   Ch'ih Yu
                 K'ua Fu

Aerial Reserve
                 Lady Torka

Reserve
                 Dragons, Dark Lady, and Master Yen

On the Mountain
                 Mr. Hu, the phoenix, Tom, Räv, and
                 birds

- **Lord Harnal moves diagonally to attack the
  hsing-t'ien in the center.**
- **Ch'ih Yu takes on the fei.**
- **Initially, K'ua Fu and Lord Trumma go
  through the gap between the hsing-t'ien and
  the fei.**

Opposite K'ua Fu and Lord Trumma, headless monsters began to dance in the center of Vatten's front line. Banging their shields against one another, they began whirling their great battle-axes so that the blades looked like deadly pinwheels. Red, baleful eyes glared from their chests and howls came from the slashlike mouths in their bellies.

"The hsing-t'ien are working themselves up into a berserk frenzy." Lady Torka frowned. "You'll have your work cut out for you, Lord Trumma."

He was busy tying his scarf around his thick neck. "I'll show them who's the better dancer and fighter."

The bloodlust of the hsing-t'ien affected the creatures behind them in the center of the second line—the chiang ling, who began to hiss and paw the dirt with their giraffe-like legs and hooves; their tongues whipped at the air and they flailed their tentacles above them.

On the left flank of Vatten's front line, next to the hsing-t'ien, were the fei, oxlike creatures who began to bellow and stomp their hooves, flailing their snakelike tails about. The single eyes in their white heads did not even blink as they butted heads and rattled their curved horns together.

Lady Torka grabbed the Dark Lady as she pointed her fan eagerly at the space left between the hsing-t'ien and the fei. "Do you see the gap, Lady? Vatten has made a mistake. He should have left the fei in the rear. Even the hsing-t'ien avoid them for fear of breathing in the toxic fumes they give off."

Ch'ih Yu lifted his spear. "Then leave the fei to us. Years of working at the forge have left our lungs like leather."

Suddenly one of the hsing-t'ien whirled and charged—not at them but at one of the chiang ling in the second line. Instantly the other chiang ling pounced to defend their comrade. Almost at the same instant, one of the fei bellowed and gored one of its fellows. Another fei attacked the chu huai who were behind on the left flank.

Vatten's orderly army started to seethe like a pudding boiling over. The squeals and howls grew even nastier and angrier until the ranks dissolved into huge shapeless clumps attacking one another.

Mr. Hu smacked his paws. "That's our ape's handiwork! The monsters' tempers are probably as strained as their bodies with the trek, the heat, and thirst. A word here, a bite there, and anger flares up as old grudges are remembered."

The misty column with Vatten inside spun like a hurricane, but it could not be everywhere at once. The orderly lines had disintegrated into a mob over which Vatten had no control. Some of the horde oozed toward the Alliance members like thirsty amoebas.

The Dark Lady's wings quivered with excitement.

"Monkey promised we'd know when it was the right time to attack. He's given us our chance. Lady Torka, can you distract both the jen-mien overhead and the chiang ling in the second line?"

"Easily," the fox said, spreading her wings so that the steel tips shone, and opening her spiked fan.

The Dark Lady drew an odd weapon from her belt, which Tom recognized from a picture in one of Mr. Hu's books. It was a *k'o*, whose sharp point could be thrust like a spear blade; but there was also a short, curved, scythe-like blade that stuck out perpendicular from the three-foot-long shaft. The weapon had fallen out of favor more than two thousand years ago. Now she pointed it at the enemy. "Lord Harnal, don't worry about their right flank. It's too disorganized to attack. You will take on the hsing-t'ien in the center instead. Lord Trumma and K'ua Fu, do you see the gap in the front line?"

The snakes rose like fire around K'ua Fu's head. "Yes, it's grown wider." The fei, intent upon battling the monsters around them, and one another, had increased the hole.

"Then go through there and strike straight at Vatten." She slashed her k'o for emphasis. "Cut off the head and the body dies." She flashed her teeth in a savage smile. "Let's save the world again, shall we?"

Lady Torka brought her wings down with a loud whump that sent her soaring upward. "For the world!" she shouted.

Her cry went up and down their thin, front rank; and they surged forward with desperate eagerness.

In Tom's history books, battles were always a series of neat lines and arrows like some geometry exercise; but this fight was nothing like that. From their ledge on the mountain side, they could see the entire battlefield: It was a jumble of images that swirled before Tom's eyes.

Single-handedly Lady Torka engaged the jen-mien, wheeling like some mad harvesting machine in the sky as the steel-tipped feathers of her outstretched wings and her spiked fan cut down the monsters. The jen-mien fell from the sky like so much ripe fruit while her warriors below swept through the chiang ling like scythes through weeds.

From the fei's mouths and nostrils, and even the pores of their bodies, rose a poisonous yellow vapor; but Ch'ih Yu and his brothers swept the fei aside as if they were dolls.

Lord Harnal and his quilled warriors were even more agile as they drove the hsing-t'ien to the side. They never stood still to fight but were always darting in from the side and back.

Forming a wedge, K'ua Fu and Lord Trumma charged into the gap in the front line. K'ua Fu's snakes danced like flames upon the sides of his head and hands. He created fear wherever he attacked because there was no defense against snakes that could stretch indefinitely and curl over shields and under armor.

And even though each had a single hind leg, Lord

Trumma and his oxen were as nimble at fighting as they were at dancing, their hides glistening like green pearls as they smashed into the very heart of Vatten's horde.

"We're winning!" Tom said, excitedly pounding his fist against a rock.

Mr. Hu frowned. "Are we? Look at the entire picture, Master Thomas."

Tom forced himself to look again, and he realized that despite their enemies' confusion, the sheer numbers were still in Vatten's favor. Though some of them still battled one another, others had closed around the Alliance. Ch'ih Yu found himself surrounded by fei and chu huai, and he and his brothers had formed a ring to shield themselves.

Now K'ua Fu and Lord Trumma's progress had ground to a halt, and it was all they could do to keep from being overwhelmed. Lady Torka and her warriors, seeing their comrades' trouble, were sweeping back and forth, trying to drive as many monsters away as they could. Lord Harnal had also seen their desperate situation and was fighting to reach them, but Vatten's monsters were putting up a stiff resistance.

"There are just too many of them," Tom said.

The Dark Lady had drawn similar conclusions. "Yes, we can't win against these odds. Are you a gambler, Guardian?"

Mr. Hu raised an eyebrow. "Stake everything on one strike?"

Master Yen drew a packet of charms from his sleeve and fanned them out as if they were the cards of a winning poker hand. "I'll measure my magic against Vatten's any day."

"And I'll match my claws," the Dragon King said, spreading them wide.

The Dark Lady swept the k'o overhead in a deadly circle. "No one stops to help anyone else. Vatten is our only goal."

"Now, to glory. Pangolin! Pangolin!" The Dragon King spread his wings, revealing the bandage on the injured one, which fortunately held as he brought them down in one great sweep and went lurching into the air. His guard rose more smoothly, sending the dust dancing like little sprites across the ground as they echoed his tribal war cry.

Spreading ebony wings, the Dark Lady launched herself upward as her warriors closed around her. Master Yen was last, mounted upon the back of one of his suan-yü. Wings clicking, the mechanical serpents shot straight into the air like helicopters.

Mistral did her best to follow them on the ground; her eyes on the dragons, she sometimes stumbled over rocks but always managed to keep on her paws.

The Dragon King led his warriors straight over the heads of the battling monsters. A shower of arrows flew upward, rattling harmlessly off their scaled bellies. The Dark Lady, close on their heels, managed to escape the next volley, but armored arms, tall as trees, suddenly shot upward, surrounding her and her escort in a grove of waving swords and axes.

"Fisher Folk," Tom cried in dismay.

Even as the Dark Lady and her companions tried to soar away, more hands grabbed their wings. They cut and sliced them with their k'os but the Fisher Folk drew them toward the ground.

Agile as hummingbirds, Master Yen's metal servants darted down to help her, but she cried, "No, go on!"

In the blink of an eye, the suan-yü leaped straight up, eluding the outstretched hands and a second volley of arrows. The Dragon King's wing gave way under the stress and he fell heavily.

Tench banked sharply. "To His Majesty," he cried as he hovered over his lord.

The other dragons would have followed, but the Dragon King struggled upright on his paws. "No, no. Never mind me. Get Vatten!" he cried.

"Yes, this way," Master Yen called from the back of his suan-yü. After milling about for a moment, Tench and the other dragons closed around him. Together they swept toward the mist that twisted and seethed angrily.

The Dragon King fought bravely, sweeping his claws in a deadly arc and swinging his tail like a club. His head shot outward on his long neck so that his fangs could wreak havoc, but for every monster he knocked down, there were two more to take its place.

His hide gashed in a dozen places, his chest heaving like bellows, his blows began to tire and he sank beneath a seething ocean of living nightmares.

"Kamsin! Kamsin!" Mistral's tribal cry rang defiantly as she drove the monsters away from the fallen king. Wheeling and leaping, she used her lashing tail and snapping fangs and slashing claws until she stood alone with him in the midst of a ring of snarling, slavering monsters.

A hsing-t'ien somersaulted through the air toward them, and Mistral's head shot toward it like a rocket.

"Hey! It's me, Monkey," the hsing-t'ien cried frantically as he narrowly dodged the clashing fangs.

"Well, how was I supposed to know, you idiot?" Mistral spat. "Ugh! It scares me to think how close I came to fouling my mouth with ape meat."

"I'm glad to see you too." Monkey laughed, changing himself back, though his robe was sadly tattered, revealing numerous wounds.

"Never mind me. Help Master Yen," the Dragon King said as he staggered to his paws and began to use his fangs. "Go, go!"

After hesitating long enough to make sure the king was holding his own now, Mistral crouched down and then vaulted high over the horde. With a nod of grudging respect to the beleaguered king, Monkey leaped into the sky and began to whip through the air as Mistral galloped on the ground toward their enemy.

In front of them, the dragons were streaking through the air toward Vatten. Just behind their rigid tails flew Master Yen. As they neared their enemy, he raised the sheaf of yellow charms so that they flapped from his fingers.

The misty column suddenly grew squatter and rounder until it formed a globe, and Master Yen flung the charms at it. They shot like arrows straight into the cloud, ripping it apart to expose Vatten himself standing in his red-scaled armor and holding his blue shield.

Around him were two dozen more jen-mien, and they rose screeching and swinging their machetes to meet the new threat.

They were no match for Master Yen and the dragons, but they provided enough of a distraction for Vatten to spread his leathery, batlike wings and flee toward the nearest band of monsters, who formed another protective circle around him.

Mistral sprang over the monsters blocking her path. "Kamsin! Kamsin!" After her flew Monkey. Mistral landed as lithe as a cat in the center of the circle and then lunged forward, jaws open, while Monkey swung his staff in a lethal blow next to her.

Tom held his breath as they struck Vatten at the same time.

And then Vatten . . . simply exploded.

Tom blinked his eyes, dazed for a moment by the flash. He saw what he thought was glittering confetti but the particles didn't behave like paper. They seemed to have a mind of their own as they spread outward like a cloud of fireflies. When they had covered the entire battlefield, they began to descend. And whenever they touched anyone, the warrior gave a cry as flesh slowly transformed into mist.

"They're dissolving!" Mr. Hu said in horror.

Monkey struggled to escape but was transformed into a small yellow cloud in mid-somersault. With one last strangled cry of "Kamsin!" Mistral became a large black cloud underneath him.

The strange thing was that the clouds still kept some of their original shape. The dragons hovered like angry storms. The misty warriors and monsters seemed more like ghosts as they swayed back and forth in pale, multicolored shapes.

"He's destroyed his own army too," Tom gasped.

Räv raised her stiletto and club with new determination. "He doesn't care. I could have told those idiots that."

"Uh-oh," Sidney said, and drew from his fur a huge fan, which he waved desperately in front of them; but fortunately the clouds never rose high enough to reach their ledge.

However, the column had now reformed into a globe. Spinning faster and faster, it shot toward the mountain like a cannon ball.

"Vatten's fooled us all. That figure we thought was him was only a decoy," Räv moaned. "He wasn't inside the column. He *is* the column."

CHAPTER FOURTEEN

The misty shapes of Monkey and Mistral tried to hurl themselves at Vatten, but the round cloud spun so that it scattered their wraithlike bodies; it was all they could do to re-form into some semblance of their former selves.

Whirling like a mad planet, Vatten sped toward the mountain. Master Yen and the dragons drifted upward with the Dark Lady and her warriors to attack him. Phantom claws and arrows struck him, only to be whipped apart like their wielders. From below, the vengeful Fisher Folk tried to grasp their former master, arms shooting up like a ghostly forest. But they, too, were dissipated, and like Mistral and Monkey, they had to fight simply to keep their misty bodies together.

Friends and foes alike had one common purpose now; striking at Vatten with silent hatred. He spun forward at head level as if inviting assaults just so he could taunt them with their helplessness.

As the red globe drew close to the mountain, the tingling at the back of Tom's neck grew so strong, he felt as if there were dozens of tiny bugs crawling under his skin. On the rocks above him, the birds chirped and squawked in alarm.

Mr. Hu gave a final tug at his cuffs and then smoothed the fur around his jowls as if he were reminding himself one last time that he was the Guardian, a symbol of civilization, and not some wild beast. "Get behind me," he murmured to Tom and Räv, and he stepped forward as calmly as if he were going to fetch the morning newspaper.

Tom tucked the phoenix within the pouch and drew the drawstrings shut. "Stay inside," he whispered.

As Vatten drew nearer and nearer, Mr. Hu said to Tom in a low voice, "When I tell you, cast the biggest wind spell you can."

"Okay," Tom said, running through the motions and words in his mind.

It was hard to concentrate as the vaporous sphere loomed over them. Ten feet in diameter, it was so close that it blocked the sun, and Tom saw that thousands of misty ribbons, wriggling like serpents, formed its surface. Their twisting bodies cast a sickly glow that sent shadows flickering this way and that. The hot air felt slimy now, and reeked of a long-dead carcass in a stagnant pool.

"At last I'll have the phoenix," a deep voice boomed from within the mist. "All the time I was hiding and recovering, I was thinking of what I would do differently if we met again, Guardian. Your claws can't touch me this time. And now I'll have my revenge for the pain and trouble you've caused me. Dissolution is too kind a death for you."

The stench from the cloud made Tom gag, and even Mr. Hu gasped before declaring, "I'll never let you have the phoenix."

The tiny snakes began to whip around faster and faster, chasing one another's tails. "Some hunter should have turned you into a rug a long time ago."

Mr. Hu's tail twitched as he growled, "Many have tried. All have failed."

The wisps were streaming so fast that the light began to blink. "A shame I couldn't have skinned you when you were in your prime. Your pelt's gotten a bit scruffy," Vatten rumbled.

Mr. Hu ears flattened tightly against his skull, but before he could lose control, Sidney spoke up. "My mother always said not to count a sale till you got the cash in paw." The rat meant to sound defiant but his voice squeaked, and the hatchet wobbled in his paw, more a danger to him than to Vatten.

Mr. Hu shoulders rose and fell as he took deep breaths and struggled to check his temper. "Your mother was a wise woman."

"And . . . and the phoenix won't do as you say anyway." Tom was so frightened that he could barely speak. "We've ordered him to obey only us—and never listen to you."

Räv threw her head back in open challenge. "No matter what you might do to us."

There was a scream of pure rage from within the ball and the serpents began to writhe as they fought one another. "I'll make you weep for what you've done."

The children could not help cringing, but Mr. Hu stood straight and tall and defiant.

Sidney squeaked, "It's either the world or nothing now, Mr. H. We're all counting on you."

Without taking his eyes off Vatten, Mr. Hu said over his shoulder, "Our visitor looks a bit hot, Master Thomas. So, a bit of your tiger magic to refresh him, please. I shall perform my own version."

Tom tried not to think about what he was doing, instead letting the long hours of practice take over; but he hadn't attempted anything this large since he had faced the Nameless One, the monster from the Dragon Kingdom. Moving his hands rapidly, he chanted the words, whipping ribbons of dust from the slope and making their clothes flap against their bodies. At the same time, he could hear Mr. Hu hissing his own spell.

The blast of wind whipped the globe with tremendous force. When the Guardian lifted his paws, his claws had changed to fire again, but this time they were as long and thin as strands of hair.

When the tiger swung his paws down, his fiery claws lashed out, crackling so close to his head that the flames singed his fur. As they shot toward Vatten, they stretched longer and thinner. And whenever one of the burning claws touched a wisp of mist, the wisp evaporated with a hiss. Mr. Hu kept swinging his paws so that his claws were in constant motion, shredding the globe to pieces.

As the air cleared, Sidney danced a little jig, his hind paws pattering on the ground. "You did it, Mr. H.!"

Little patches of mist lingered in the air, and Mr. Hu continued to flail at them, but his eyes and nose seemed to be hunting for something else. "Not until I destroy his heart," he grunted. "As long as that survives, he can always renew himself."

Tom scanned the rocks and thought he spotted a scarlet glint. "Is that it?" he asked, pointing.

Threads of mist streamed toward it, quickly hiding the glittering object from view.

"Yes," Mr. Hu said. But even as the tiger swept his flaming claws downward, the gathering mist had already swelled to the size of a basketball and the flames slid harmlessly off.

In a split second, the globe had grown to the height of Mr. Hu.

Räv urged Tom, "Give him another shot."

But the blast of wind only shredded an outer layer, sending the mist shooting in all directions like missiles. Spinning around, Mr. Hu swept the children toward him. There was a hissing sound wherever the vapor struck earth or rock, burning for a moment like a drop of acid. Sidney cried out as one smacked against him and there was an acrid smell as it burned his pelt. Mr. Hu roared in pain as the bits burned clothing and fur but he refused to budge; and the children and the phoenix, safely hidden behind the tiger's living shield, were safe.

"You won't catch me with the same trick twice," Vatten taunted. "Your magic's no match for mine."

They saw that the mist had formed into the shape Vatten had used in Chinatown, but his body and armor shimmered and the outline kept changing slightly. His red hair, when it had definition, looked like a wriggling nest of worms and his tusks writhed like snakes. In his empty eye sockets, they could see strings of angry blue lights writhing.

The one thing that seemed solid was his necklace, made up of raw amber lumps and a sky-blue stone.

Mr. Hu's lips moved as he drew magical signs that left a golden afterglow, creating an intricate web of light. The air felt electric with the powerful enchantment—as if they were within a thunder cloud about to discharge a lightning bolt.

Vatten's mouth curled up in a sneer. "Do your worst,

Guardian. And then I'll add your soul to my necklace. Do you recognize these?" He hooked a finger under the necklace and lifted it from his chest so that the stones sparkled in the flickering light from his eye sockets. "You should. They're your kin. You've frustrated me so much, I paid your clan a little visit."

Mr. Hu broke off the spell. "My clan!"

Vatten pursed his lips as he played with the yellow rocks. "A pity that I exterminated them. I do *so* love tiger amber and where will I find more after I kill you? I didn't bother to string the cubs. They were mere pebbles." Vatten pinched the largest one between his fingers. "This one was their chief. She screamed the loudest before I took her soul."

"The cubs too?" Mr. Hu snarled. "You—!" In his fury, he could not even form words but made only yowling noises.

Tom could feel the tiger blood pounding in his head as a wild hatred rose in him, but *now was no time to lose control.* "Mr. Hu, use your magic," he tried to remind his master.

"Yes-s-s," Mr. Hu hissed, struggling to control himself.

"And," Vatten drawled, "do you see this stone?" He tapped the sky-blue gem. "This is your predecessor."

"But we saw the Ghost Cart that took my grandmother to the afterlife!" Tom protested, horrified by Vatten's boast.

"It was premature." Vatten laughed.

When Tom had nearly died after their last battle, the

Ghost Cart had also come for him, but Mr. Hu had managed to keep it from carrying his apprentice away. Could Vatten have done the same thing to his grandmother and kept her alive? The boy alternated between hope that she still lived and the horror that she was a prisoner of her mortal enemy.

"I knew she might seek death to escape my revenge"—Vatten could not resist boasting—"so I gave my creatures the means to imprison her within this stone. She's fully conscious but can do nothing to stop my triumph."

"How dare you torture Mistress Lee!" howled Mr. Hu. Gone was the gentlemanly tiger and the wizard steeped in Lore. Manners and wisdom had evaporated before his white-hot rage. Falling to all fours, Mr. Hu became a wild beast. Even his suit seemed too small for his body as his powerful muscles threatened to tear the cloth.

His tail lashing, his ears tight against his skull, his eyes narrowed to slits, Mr. Hu gave a ferocious roar and then pounced with all the power in his legs. His claws swept in slashes that would have torn any other creature apart but passed harmlessly through Vatten's sides.

"Whatever made a dumb beast like you think you could be the Guardian?" Vatten taunted. Even though his fist still looked like mist, it knocked Mr. Hu to the ground.

With a yowl, the tiger leaped to his paws and sprang again with open jaws. His head twisted from side to side but his fangs only closed on vapor, and as quick as he whipped Vatten's torso, it regained its shape again.

With the back of his hand, Vatten tossed Mr. Hu against the rocks. "What can a tiger know about magic? You fell for the simplest of illusions. Do you think I would really soil my hands with such lowly creatures?" When he whipped the necklace over his head, the amber changed back into the mist it really was. The necklace glittered like a shining scarlet rope as he flung it. As soon as it touched the rising tiger, it wound itself round and round, pulling Mr. Hu's limbs tight against his body so that the tiger crashed to the ground.

CHAPTER FIFTEEN

Mr. Hu thrashed upon the ground, twisting his head to bite at the scarlet bindings.

Tom growled, "Mr. Hu!" He would have raced to help the Guardian, but Sidney grabbed his arm. "No, Tom. It's up to us now."

Tom knew the rat was right. All he could do was watch Mr. Hu struggle helplessly.

Vatten's empty sockets gazed down at the fallen tiger. "I do hope it feels as uncomfortable as it looks."

At first, only snarls issued from Mr. Hu's throat, but then he recovered enough of his reason to ignore Vatten and call to his apprentice instead: "Master Thomas, use your m—!"

"Your bindings are too loose if you can still yowl." Vatten's nebulous hand made a pass above the tiger and immediately he stiffened and began to gasp.

"Which spell, Mr. Hu?" Tom called to the tiger, but Mr. Hu lay still, eyes wide and mouth open as he struggled just to breathe in his tightened bonds.

"Do not hurt Grandpa!" the phoenix shrieked. The noise had made him so curious that he had forced the taut drawstrings of the pouch apart with his head.

With his foot, Vatten turned the strangling tiger to face the mountain. "You can watch me destroy the world, and know that you've failed."

He didn't seem to think the children and rat were a threat. Turning away from them, he raised his arms, and his eye sockets flashed with an intense, steely light. Instantly Tom's mouth felt parched and his skin was so dry that it began to itch, and he grew thirstier and itchier. When he looked at the pool, he saw that all the water had evaporated.

"He must be drawing the moisture from everything," Tom managed to croak.

"Including us." Sidney had fallen to his knees. "Jeepers, now I know what a cookie feels like when it's baked."

The water sucked from the surroundings slowly solidified in Vatten's hands, forming a silvery halberd with a spike at one end and a large axe-like blade sticking out from the shaft.

Terrified, Räv grabbed Tom. "Stop him!" she said through cracked lips.

Vatten laughed. "What can a half-beast like you do?"

211

A low growl rasped in Tom's dry throat. The Guardian looked desperately at his apprentice, trying to tell him, but all he could do was wheeze. The sight of his tormented master made the boy so angry that his desire for revenge was as physical as his thirst. He wanted to spring at the monster and tear him apart. He'd show Vatten just what a half-tiger could do.

By now Vatten's halberd had grown to fifty yards in length and yet he handled it as easily as a stick. When he brought the blade down upon the slope, it gouged a huge gash like the hardest steel. The birds of the Alliance shrieked as they flapped into the air, and boulders came crashing down upon the spot where they had been.

He couldn't give in to his tiger's blood, Tom told himself. He had to use his mind instead. What magic did Mr. Hu want him to use?

"Stop me, half beast, if you can." Vatten mocked him and sliced the mountain again with a thunderous crash.

The phoenix was quivering. "What happened to Grandpa?"

Räv jabbed a finger at Vatten. "He hurt your grandpa. So hurt him."

The phoenix jumped when Vatten cut at the slope a third time. "Mama, he scares me. Papa says hurt him. Can I?"

Tom was so furious that he was trembling. The tiger in him demanded exactly what Räv had urged; but in the back of his mind he saw his grandmother, and behind her all her predecessors stretching in a long line back into the shadows of the past. To give in to temptation now would betray everything for which the Guardians had stood, fought, and died. For thousands of years, noble creatures had guarded against the abuse of the phoenix's power. And with Mr. Hu fallen, his apprentice had to be the Guardian in his stead once again, and this time for the greatest of decisions.

So, though his voice shook, Tom replied, "No, don't hurt him."

Through his eye sockets, they could see the silvery lights whirling madly as Vatten's face twisted into a crazy smile. "I knew you wouldn't be brave enough to use the phoenix. You're the worst of two species—a human without wits and a tiger without courage."

The next blow of his halberd against the mountain knocked both children off their feet.

Rising on her elbow, Räv pointed at herself and pleaded, "Don't listen to Mama. Listen to Papa. The whole world's at stake."

Again Vatten struck the slope; this time, the mountain shook with the aftershock, sending an avalanche of rocks sliding downward on all sides.

The phoenix's beak dropped open as he stared and then he begged Tom, "Mama, please. Let me hurt him like Papa says."

As Tom gazed down at the bird's sullen black eyes, he realized a terrible truth: The temptation of power was as great for the phoenix as for anyone else. Guardians had to protect their charge against his natural instincts.

Tom had seen how vindictive the little bird could be when he was lost and angry. If Tom told the phoenix to use his power now, what would happen during the next emergency? It would go on and on, each time getting easier to give in, until the phoenix would use his power whenever someone simply upset him. How long would it be before the phoenix himself became as bad as Vatten?

Tom couldn't allow that to happen. The phoenix truly was his son, and no parent would willingly allow their child to become evil.

Räv clenched her fists in frustration as she shouted at the phoenix. "Are we family or aren't we? Stop Vatten!"

The bird clutched his head between his wings. "I don't know. I don't know. Papa says hurt. I want to hurt. But Mama says not to hurt." Tom felt his own insides twist to see the phoenix in such agony. Love, anger, and fear warred within him.

"Hey, kiddo," said Sidney, "you gotta let the canary whomp Vatten. You owe it to the world." He swung his hatchet in illustration.

Tom cringed as Vatten struck the mountain again, but he shook his head. "You can't commit a wrong to stop another."

"You're a coward just like Vatten says," Räv spat at him.

Stung by her words, Tom rose, but it was hard to keep his feet. "I . . . I'm willing to fight him."

"Well, if that's the only way." Sidney sighed, hefting up his hatchet. "I'll pitch in too."

Räv lifted her stiletto over her shoulder, the point between her fingertips. "If all these warriors couldn't stop him, how can you expect to?" She threw it at Vatten, but it whistled harmlessly through his misty torso and he didn't appear to notice.

"See?" she said, exasperated. "We can't do a thing against him."

That seemed true enough, and yet the Guardian had thought of a way. But what? Tom ran through all the spells he knew, but the wind spell was the only one that had done any damage to Vatten and the monster had come up with countermagic.

"Flee, Your Highness," Mistress Quick urged. Tom twisted his head to see the little bird upon his shoulder. "It's a mistake to stay any longer."

Mistake! Maybe Mr. Hu hadn't been trying to tell him to use magic. Maybe he'd been trying to say *mistake*. But which one? He made so many. And then he remembered. "I could kiss you, Mistress Quick!"

"Oh, no, I couldn't," the little bird said, flustered. "What would Master Thick think?"

"I'm sorry." Tom smiled. "It's just that you've given us a chance to win."

The yellow-and-black bird's beak gaped open and she nodded her head firmly. "Then I'll fight at His Highness's side."

She had given Tom another idea and he looked up at the flock of panicked birds circling overhead. "Will the others attack too?"

"I can't answer for them," she said. "Each would have to decide if summoned by His Highness."

The phoenix twisted his head, perplexed. "Mama said not to hurt."

"You can't use your power because it is so strong," the boy explained, "but that doesn't mean the rest of us can't fight."

Sidney's fur began to hum. "I'm with you, Tom," he said, rising a few inches from the ground, his outline shimmering.

"I knew it was stupid to join a family." Räv shrugged. "But I might as well go on being stupid."

"Would you please call your subjects?" Tom asked the little bird.

"Excuse me," the phoenix called to the birds wheeling overhead. "Will you . . . please fight him," he said, pointing at their enemy.

Vatten laughed harshly as he held his halberd over his head. "What can they do?"

"Alone, very little," the pi fang called from above, "but together we serve our king."

With a flap of his wings, the falcon dove out of the sky. "Come, brothers and sisters!" he cried.

The pi fang followed, booming like a feathered drum; and from the largest to the smallest, the frightened birds answered their king and swept after the falcon and pi fang, slicing down like a living guillotine.

Vatten altered his swing in midstroke, swinging it toward the flock instead of the mountain. "I'll destroy you all."

But just as Vatten was about to strike the flock, Mistress Quick darted straight into his face, pecking with her small beak and tearing with her tiny claws. Caught by surprise, he hadn't prepared a protective spell. Wherever she struck, she whipped ribbons of mist to the left and the right. Even though the ribbons constantly re-formed into his face, the determined bird kept Vatten from seeing clearly.

With an angry scream, he dropped the halberd, which burst into a low rolling fog upon contact with the slope. And he flailed instead at the little bird until he swatted her to the side.

As Vatten straightened furiously, his face reassembling, the phoenix's army smashed into him like a feathery fist, throats shrieking like desperate ghosts, beaks and claws and wings ripping his cloudy shape into shreds.

And as quickly as Vatten tried to regain his shape, the

whirling flock of birds sent the mist swirling away again.

"Come on," Tom roared. Now was the time to give in to his tiger's blood, and he found it so easy and strangely pleasant to surrender to his fury at last. It burned in him like fire as he bounded forward on legs that were as powerful as springs. One hand covered the phoenix protectively as he scrambled on, heedless of the bruises and scrapes.

Sidney hummed on his left, skimming over the now damp rocks. Räv stumbled on his right. "If we live through this, I'm going to pound your stubborn head, Tom."

They could hear Vatten's furious screams rising from within the ball of attacking birds; but the moment of victory wouldn't last. One moment the phoenix's army was swarming around him, the next there was a bright flash of light and birds were thrown in all directions, tumbling beak over tail.

They were only a couple of yards away now and Vatten seemed to tower over them, his body and face resuming their shape again. Light flashed from his eyes like sparks off steel, and his hair rose around his head like some evil banner.

Taking a breath, Tom worked his spell, aiming straight at Vatten's heart. But it was not as easy to repeat a mistake as to make it in the first place.

"Oh, Tom," Räv groaned as Vatten's chest merely turned pink.

Eyes blazing from his misty head, Vatten reached his hands toward Tom before he could try another spell. "I'll tear you apart."

Suddenly Sidney buzzed over the boy, swinging his hatchet back and forth like a furry saw. "Take this, you gasbag!"

Vatten shouted as it sliced through his neck. But even before his neck returned to its original shape, his fist sent the rat tumbling against a boulder, where he lay limp.

Sidney's sacrifice, however, had bought enough precious seconds for Tom to try his enchantment again. His blood raced, filling him with the raw, wild energy of the earth itself; and the magic straining within his body was an untamed beast wanting to escape its cage. As Tom roared out the chant, the magic leaped from his fingertips like a tiger pouncing upon its prey.

"What color will I be this time?" Vatten sneered, but the next moment his smile changed to a puzzled frown as the mist that was his chest solidified into a patch of pink ice.

"Gotcha!" Holding her club in both hands, Räv struck at the now solid target.

Vatten gaped as cracks spread across the spot where the girl's club, now splintering, had hit. "No!"

Yanking his own club from his belt and roaring so loudly that his throat ached, Tom swung with all his might.

The blow shattered Vatten's chest, and the momentum

carried the club forward until it struck something so hard it numbed Tom's arms and the club shattered like Räv's had.

Vatten stared down stunned as the icy fragments of his torso rained down upon the backs of Tom's hands. Within the cavity, Tom saw that his club had hit Vatten's heart; and even as he watched, it disintegrated into dozens of needlelike shards.

Instantly, Vatten's body began to lose its form. Arms, legs, and torso spread outward into a shapeless cloud of bloody steam that vanished in the hot, dry air.

Vatten's head was the last part to lose its shape. The creature who would have destroyed the world opened his mouth one last time but no scream came from the dark hole . . . and then even his head was gone.

CHAPTER SIXTEEN

Tom stood blinking, amazed that he was still alive, as
the birds wheeled overhead singing in triumph.

"Mama, Mama?" the phoenix peeped.

From the urgent squirming beneath his fingers, Tom
realized he had both hands cupped protectively over the
pouch.

"It's okay," he said, stroking the frightened bird. He
felt quite content to just lie there and stare up at the sky,
which was quickly clearing to a deep, bright blue.

"Oog, speak for yourself," Sidney said as he stumbled
over. He was cradling his left paw in his right, and there
was a kink in his tail.

Räv was on her knees, coughing. "Ugh, I think I
inhaled some of Vatten."

The rat wriggled his snout in agreement. "He'll never
make a great cologne."

Worried, the phoenix began to poke Tom's chest. "Mama, you are hurt?"

The boy unclasped his hands from the pouch, and the little red head poked out. "See? Mama's fine."

The phoenix swiveled his head. "Papa?"

Too busy trying to spit out the taste of Vatten, Räv only nodded to indicate she was all right.

"Uncle Sidney?" the phoenix asked.

"It takes more than sewer gas to kill a rat, kiddo." Sidney paused as he tried to straighten out his tail. "Hey, you called me by my name. Have you been teasing me all this time?"

The phoenix simply smiled. "Maybe."

Affectionately Tom smoothed down an unruly tuft of feathers. "Can't have you looking like that for your subjects."

Then he looked around. "What about Mistress Quick?"

"With her broken wing, she won't be flying for a while," Mr. Hu said as he limped toward them. His scarlet bindings clung to his clothing as misty threads. Cupped in his paw was the wounded bird.

"Master Thick will be ever so worried," she chirped, peering over his claws. Mistress Quick had lost a patch of feathers from the left side of her head and one eye was swollen shut.

"We'll send him a message," Mr. Hu said. "Or better yet, we'll fetch him so he can fuss over our hero." With his free paw, he brushed the mist from his clothes, and the blue stone clattered to the ground. "You kept your head when I didn't, Master Thomas. He knew that my beastly temper was my weakness and used a simple illusion to trick me."

Tom stared at the spot where Vatten had fallen. All that remained of him were puddles of melting ice and a few red wisps, which slowly disappeared. As the boy gazed down at the battlefield, he felt no triumph, only a great sense of loss.

Mr. Hu gazed in the same direction. "Let's say farewell to our friends, shall we?"

"Yeah," Sidney sighed, "before the next wind blows them away."

Tom nodded mutely, on the verge of tears. Together they left the ledge and threaded their way down the slope to the plain. They passed through a ring of monsters around Lord Trumma—though it was hard to be sure it was him, as his misty shape had already lost much of its definition. As they walked on, they saw what they thought were Ch'ih Yu and his brothers fighting to reach his dancing rival.

"Sad," the phoenix murmured.

Tom soothed the little bird by stroking the tiny head

with his thumb. Wherever his eye traveled, there were hundreds of stories that were part of that day's desperate struggle. Lady Torka. Lord Harnal. K'ua Fu. The dragons.

They finally found Mistral floating like a great black cloud.

"She's fighting to keep her form," Mr. Hu said. Her features were lost as the cloud drifted and expanded, but then the cloud regained its shape to reveal her face. Her mouth seemed to be moving as if she were trying to say good-bye. "She died as bravely as she lived," he observed.

"She never gave up," Räv said admiringly.

"Dragons are too stupid to know when they've lost," a familiar voice said.

Tom whirled around to see the transparent form of Monkey slowly becoming more solid. "You can talk?"

The ape raised a pale paw through which they could see the landscape, and then used it to scratch his head. "What do you know?"

"I should have known your mouth would be the last part of you to go," another familiar voice grumbled.

Sidney turned and poked one of Mistral's ebony legs. It dimpled like rubber rather than scattering like mist. "I think you're getting more solid too," he told her.

The tiger threw back his head and let out a triumphant roar. "Of course! The spell ended with Vatten's death."

With their strength and energy, the dragons solidified

at a faster pace than the other creatures, but all around the misty garden ghostly shrubs were coalescing into warriors and monsters again. But as many as there were who now stood wondering at what had happened, there were many others who lay unmoving in the dirt.

All the fight had gone out of Vatten's monstrous army when they materialized. Weapons and armor were cast on the ground, and the monsters knelt, touching their foreheads to the dirt in surrender. They were paroled into the custody of Lady Torka and the other rebels.

Mr. Hu refused to answer any questions until everyone was able to listen, insisting that he had the energy to tell the tale only once. When friends and foes had finally gathered around the tiger, he told them briefly but clearly of how Vatten had been defeated.

When he was done, the Dark Lady was the first to speak. "You've brought even greater glory to the Guardianship." When she bowed her head, everyone else followed her example.

As he straightened, K'ua Fu raised his fists, the serpents wriggling happily like giant sea anemones. "A cheer for Master Hu!"

But, before the others could even gather their breath, the tiger beat the air with his paws and roared, "No, no. I failed." He pivoted, his tail whipping around. "We owe our salvation to them." He indicated Sidney, Tom, and Räv.

"You've shown me you're quality, girl—I mean, Ambassador," Lord Harnal said, bowing his head to Räv in formal apology.

"And me," Lord Trumma agreed. "Will you ever forgive us?"

"It's Tom and Sidney's doing as much as mine," Räv said, embarrassed by the praise.

Tom also felt self-conscious as all eyes turned toward them. At his feet the phoenix's loyal subjects were perched with many broken wings and limbs still to be tended. He put his hand beneath Mr. Hu's paw, which still held Mistress Quick, and lifted it so everyone could see her. "No, it was the birds that won the day!" Tom's roar carried across the plain. Sometimes it was useful to have a tiger's voice. "Without them, we could never have gotten near Vatten."

The injured bird was surprised by all the attention. "We only kept faith with His Highness."

"Thank you," the phoenix said, emerging from the pouch. He looked from Mistress Quick to the flock around him. "Thank you all."

The Dark Lady smiled at the birds. "The whole world thanks you."

Ch'ih Yu laughed as he stared down at his hamlike fist. "I can crush a boulder with one blow; but these little birds did what I couldn't."

Master Yen dipped his head. "We are in your debt."

And everywhere the great warriors bowed to the humblest creatures in their ranks—which flustered poor Mistress Quick so much that, for once, the bird was speechless.

"All of you will have places of honor at the victory feast," Lord Harnal promised, his quill tips clinking as he lowered his head again.

"But we won't celebrate until we've hunted down what's left of Vatten's followers," Master Yen said with a rueful glance at Mr. Hu. "We don't want anyone taking his place."

Lord Trumma tested his hind leg. "Yes, let's make sure that none of them set themselves up as the next Vatten. This victory was too near a thing."

Lord Harnal nodded. "And this time, we work together. No more suspicion or mistrust."

Ch'ih Yu fingered some new dents in his armor. "I don't think I'll survive a Third Battle of the Imperfect Mountain."

The Dragon King cleared his throat. "We should mourn the fallen first." He pointed a claw at a giant moth that flapped toward them; its pale gray wings were spotted with brown shapes resembling skulls.

"It's the Ghost Cart," Monkey said, slipping off his cap as he gazed upward.

Piping and cawing in fear, the birds rose in an explosion of wings; and those who could not, slipped in closer to their king for protection.

"That's scary," the phoenix murmured, hunching his shoulders.

Trembling, Tom began to take off the pouch and hand it to Mr. Hu.

He felt the Guardian's reassuring paw on his shoulder. "It's all right, Master Thomas. I've shared my blood with you—and with it some of my soul. The Ghost Cart has no claim on you anymore."

As the Ghost Cart circled slowly over the battlefield, little ribbons of light rose from the dead and hung suspended, as if dazed for a moment. The Ghost Cart banked and spiraled upward, and the streamers spun faster and faster.

"They've become butterflies," Tom breathed.

One by one, they spread their wings and flapped them, tentatively at first and then with delight, enjoying their freedom. Tom felt his own heart growing lighter when he saw how joyfully they fluttered over the battlefield. Then they darted toward the Ghost Cart, whose wings pulsed as it took in each heroic soul and began to glow brilliantly.

When it had taken each and every one of them, it banked and flew toward the west, beating its shimmering wings.

Monster and hero were silent until it was out of sight.

All the travel and fighting had caught up with the tiger, and he leaned heavily on his apprentice. "Thank Heaven, it's done and we're still alive."

Tom felt almost as weary as his master. Tiger magic was powerful but hard on the body.

"I knew you had it in you, Hu."

Tom turned his head and his jaw dropped. "Grand-mom?"

His grandmother was picking her way down the slope, still in the dress and apron she was wearing when Vatten's monsters had attacked her house.

"So Vatten's stone wasn't an illusion after all?" Mr. Hu gasped.

"I taught you better than that." Mistress Lee smiled. "Vatten took delight in hiding the truth among his lies. I saw and heard everything he did from my prison." She gave the tiger a hug but she reserved the biggest one for her grandson. "And I knew you had it in you, too, Tom."

As he felt her arms wrap around him, Tom rested his head against her familiar shoulder. "This feels like a dream."

She caught the glint of a shining speck and tilted her head back. "What's that on your face?"

Mr. Hu cleared his throat. "The mark of the Empress's favor."

Almost in awe, she touched Tom's cheek just below the glittering scale. "You visited her and lived to tell the tale?"

"It was the only way to save his life," Mr. Hu said apologetically.

"Who is she?" the phoenix interrupted as he pointed his beak toward Mistress Lee.

"Your great-grandmom," Tom explained as he held the phoenix up for a better look.

Mistress Lee looked startled but pleased. "Great-grandmom?"

Mr. Hu scratched a jowl. "It's a long story."

"And an interesting one, I'm sure." Mistress Lee laughed and gazed at the bird with undisguised joy and excitement. After all these centuries, she and Mr. Hu were the first Guardians to gaze upon their charge without his shell. "Well, I'm sorry you had so much trouble. If I hadn't been in my prison, maybe I could have headed it off."

With a flutter of his wings, the phoenix flew over to her shoulder and brushed his feathery head against her cheek. "It doesn't matter. We're family now."

Mistress Lee turned to the silver-haired girl. "And you must be Räv. Your name was on Vatten's lips many times."

The girl eyed her cautiously. "Probably when he was cursing," she mumbled.

But Mistress Lee was not one to stand on ceremony and she hugged Räv as well. "I saw you fighting with my grandson. Well done." And though the girl stiffened at the first contact, she eventually returned the embrace.

230

Mistress Lee already knew the rest of their companions, including Sidney from whom she had once bought a dubious hand lotion.

"Sorry about the warts, Mrs. L.," Sidney said, toeing the dirt as he squirmed. "But you should always read the fine print on the label."

"I would have needed a microscope," Mistress Lee said with mock sternness, and Sidney cautiously edged behind Tom. "But since you're a hero, all's forgiven," she said and blew him a kiss.

"Yeah, who'd a thunk it," Sidney said relieved.

Then she greeted the Dragon King and the rest of the warriors.

Lady Torka spread her wings as she dipped her head. "I'm glad we are on the same side, Mistress Lee. We lost many friends in the assault on your house. You were a worthy adversary. Perhaps too worthy."

Mistress Lee was about to reply, when they heard a thunderous crack.

"What's that?" the phoenix asked anxiously from her shoulder.

"I don't know," she said, looking around, puzzled.

Tom thought it had begun to snow, but then he realized the swirling flakes were blue.

"Look, Mama, pretty," the phoenix piped happily.

Alarmed, Mr. Hu tilted back his head. "It's the sky,"

he growled. "It's breaking."

Tom gazed upward and saw a thin line creeping across the heavens. As he watched, it began to widen, and beyond it was a darkness that was blacker than anything he had ever seen.

CHAPTER SEVENTEEN

At first, the disintegrating sky fell in a fine grit, but the pieces increased in volume until they were large clusters of blue crystals the size of pebbles. The points stung wherever they touched, and Tom couldn't help flinching as they rattled down.

Instinctively Mistress Lee had taken the phoenix from her shoulder and was cradling him against her stomach.

Mr. Hu bent over her as further protection. "Find shelter!" he roared.

The order was hardly necessary as everyone tried to hide under cliffs and overhangs or even dig their way under boulders. Only the dragons, confident in their armored hides, remained standing as they anxiously gazed up at the crumbling sky. The fallen powder was dyeing the water in the pool a deep blue.

"Come to me," Mistral called to her friends as

she raised her good wing.

Tom and Räv huddled beneath her great bulk along with Mistress Lee, Mr. Hu, Sidney, and Monkey.

Rubbing some sky dust from his eye, the tiger growled, "Vatten must have done just enough damage to bring the sky down."

"He's won after all," Räv said, looking close to tears, her face powdered blue from the dust.

Sidney peeked out from underneath Mistral's wing as little blue shards tapped against it. "This is going to take more than glue."

They all looked hopefully at Mistress Lee, but she shook her head. "It's beyond my magic."

"And mine," Master Yen confessed from beneath the protection of his servants' wings.

"Grandpop can fix?" the frightened phoenix asked the tiger.

"It would take a far older and greater magic than anyone here has," Mr. Hu said, and turned his head to gaze at Tom.

Tom was wondering why everyone was staring at him, when he began to feel a sudden warmth on his cheek. He touched it and realized it was the scale, growing hotter and hotter.

"Mama, you're like a star." The phoenix gasped in amazement, as the scale began to glow with a soft yellow light.

Tom realized that sealing the sky was in the power of only one person. "The Empress said I could use this to summon her. She repaired the sky once. Maybe she can do it again."

"Calling her is too dangerous," Mistress Lee said. "I won't allow it."

She ducked instinctively as a jagged piece of sky crashed against the slope and bounced away. Mistral started to sag as larger fragments thumped against her.

"Yikes!" Sidney gulped. From somewhere in his fur, he had pulled out a bicycle helmet and was trying to strap it on. "If ever there was a time, this is it."

Mr. Hu rumbled somberly. "If she helps us, it will be in her own way and perhaps not to our liking."

"Do we have a choice?" Monkey flinched as a chunk the size of a bowling ball crashed next to them.

Tom thought of how much he had come to love all of them and wouldn't be able to bear if they were harmed. "I'm sorry, Grandmom. The Empress gave it to me and I think that means she left the decision to me. I'll . . . I'll take on whatever trouble comes."

"But we've just found one another again," his grandmother protested.

"Mistress Lee, I can't stand this pounding much longer." Mistral shuddered as another big piece shattered against her back. The dragon's powerful legs were buckling from the impact.

"I'm not making any sacrifice you weren't willing to," Tom reminded her. "Mr. Hu said that sometimes Guardians have to make tough choices."

"Hu's taught you too well, I think." His grandmother blinked back tears. "You've grown up so fast."

Tom took the phoenix from her arms. "You listen to the rest of your family if something happens to me."

"I go where Mama goes," the phoenix said stubbornly.

"You . . . you won't be able to follow me this time." Tom swallowed.

"No, Mama." The bird embraced him, pressing the downy wings against his face.

Tom placed a hand against the phoenix's back for a moment, feeling how soft he was.

"Mama doesn't want to go, but he has to," the boy choked.

Mr. Hu squeezed Tom's shoulder. "She said to plant it in the ground. Then slap the earth and call her."

Regretfully, Tom handed the phoenix to Räv. Then Tom pulled at the scale, which had clung to his cheek as if glued, but now came off easily in his fingers and cast a soft, pleasant glow.

Scraping a hole in the rocky soil, he placed it at the bottom and then swept the dirt back over it. He slapped his palm on the ground and called, "Come, Empress Nü Kua." He remembered to add "Please."

They waited breathlessly. After several minutes, when

nothing had happened, Tom sighed. "Maybe I didn't do it right." He glanced at the Guardian and his grandmother.

Mr. Hu shrugged, stroking his whiskers thoughtfully. "There is nothing in the Lore about summoning the Empress."

"Because no one would dare to," Mistress Lee said with a worried look at her grandson.

Suddenly the ground began to rumble. From all around them, birds twittered and monsters howled alike in terror; and the world's mightiest warriors and wizards shouted in fright, "Earthquake!"

With a gigantic grinding noise, the pond cracked open. As water, dirt, and rock cascaded down into the chasm, they heard a sleepy voice echoing petulantly from the depths, "This had better be important to wake me up."

There was the sound of rattling chariot wheels, growing louder until her team of dragons vaulted upward from the gap. Tom had met plenty of dragons in their undersea kingdom, but as ancient as they were, they were infants compared to the Empress's. Her dragons had been born at the creation of the world and were as different from their descendants as the first *Australopithecus* were from modern humans. These dragons were smaller than Mistral but there was something wild in their eyes, for they had not had millennia of civilization to tame them. When they fought, their aim would be not just to kill, but to devour.

The four seemed more than a match for all the monsters and warriors upon the mountain, yet they pranced together as a team in a harness of yellow mist. The inner pair had tall, curling horns while the outer pair had wings. Behind them, they hauled a chariot as gray as a storm cloud and striped with gold like lightning bolts.

Tom had been unconscious when he had been brought before the Empress, but from everything he had heard about her, he had been expecting some creature even more terrifying than Vatten. So he was surprised to see that the driver who controlled this dreadful team looked like a girl of sixteen. She was clad in a gown of golden, iridescent scales, and her black hair had been piled into intricate serpentine coils. When the chariot had rolled to a halt before them, she climbed down. Little wisps of yellow vapor clung to her ankles like golden anklets and a soft yellow light surrounded her, against which the falling rocks bounced off harmlessly.

The Dark Lady gasped. "The Empress." Hastily she knelt, touching her forehead against the dirt.

As warriors and wizards and dragons everywhere bowed to her, the Empress wriggled her hand. "Yes, yes, I'm glad you still remember your manners, but let's not stand on formality."

A blue boulder smashed into the slope, shattering into a dozen huge fragments that ricocheted off her protective aura. The Empress glanced at the pieces as if they were no more than gnats and then frowned skyward. "Well, I suppose that patch was going to come undone sometime." She lowered her eyes to Mistress Lee, Mr. Hu, and their companions; then her guardian light expanded until it had surrounded them as well. "Where's the boy? Only he could have called me."

Now that her friends were safe, Mistral stepped back. Tom tried to stand up, but his knees had turned to gelatin.

From the cradle of Räv's arms, the phoenix gazed at the Empress. "Pretty," he piped.

When the Empress smiled, she looked even younger. "It's been ages, Your Highness," she said, bowing to the phoenix. "Not that I am unhappy to meet you, but your birth seems premature. Or has the world found peace?"

"It was"—Mr. Hu hesitated as the Dragon King did his best to imitate a boulder—"an accident, Your Highness."

She arched an eyebrow ironically. "That must have been some accident." A chunk of sky as large as a house crashed on the mountain slope and called her attention back to the crack, which was widening, revealing more and more of the terrible darkness. "Well, I guess we'd better stop this."

Tom finally found his voice. "Please save us."

The Empress laughed as she set her hands on her hips. "But it's *you* who'll save *me*."

Tom wondered if she were playing another one of her infamous pranks. "But how?"

She strolled over to him. "My feelings are hurt. You don't remember when we first met?"

"I was asleep," Tom confessed. "I'm sorry."

"I won't ever forget," Sidney muttered with a shudder. "It gave me the heebie-jeebies."

The sharp ears of the Empress missed nothing. "And well it should, rodent. But I meant the time when the world was still young."

"But I'm not that old," Tom said, puzzled.

"Great souls are reborn, just as the phoenix is," the Empress said, smiling. "On that other terrible day when Kung Kung lay dead and the heavens cracked open, I took five stones, each of a different color, and fused them together to weld the sky shut."

"And . . . we are the five stones?" Mr. Hu asked, looking around at his friends.

The Empress nodded as she held out her hands. "You were drawn to one another by bonds forged in other lives long ago. Now will you help me again?"

This time Tom's legs felt strong as he stood up. Mr. Hu and Monkey rose with him. Mistral nudged the crouching rat. "Sidney," she hissed.

"I'm getting up," the rat said as he wobbled upright.

The Empress put a hand on Tom's arm. Her skin was cool and dry. "Will you help me willingly, Spirit of Wood?"

Tom nodded mutely.

"Spirit of Fire?" she asked Mr. Hu, who bowed his head silently.

She turned to Mistral. "Spirit of Water?"

The dragon dipped her long, elegant neck.

"Spirit of Metal?" she asked Monkey.

The ape simply smiled in answer.

Sidney was the last and he trembled when he felt the weight of the Empress's full attention. "Spirit of Earth?" she asked the rat.

"I . . . I don't suppose we could make a deal," Sidney squeaked.

"No," the Empress replied firmly.

"I guess we're partners to the end," the rat said, trying to grin bravely at his friends.

Clutching the phoenix, Räv looked from Tom to Mr. Hu. "You can't leave me alone like this," she protested.

"No, Mama, no," the phoenix cheeped.

Mistress Lee put her hands on Räv's. "They're doing what they must."

"As must we all." The Empress closed her eyes, spread her hands, and turned her face skyward. Her lips moved as she whispered a spell in a language never meant for any human voice.

Sounds slipped from her lips like water spreading across the barrenness, growing louder until they became the waves of oceans. And her teeth ground together like mountains rubbing against one another as they climbed out of earth and water. Suddenly, throat-wrenching howls and shrill yips crawled forth from her mouth like foul beetles.

The hair on Tom's neck rose, and Räv had fallen to the ground, curled up on her side, as she cradled the phoenix. Everywhere, monster and warrior and dragon pressed themselves against the dirt as if trying to hide from the Empress.

And just when Tom thought he could not stand the sounds anymore, the loveliest notes rose from the Empress's mouth, lilting cries like a bird soaring through the air, or light dancing upon the back of a silvery river as it races joyfully to the sea. Tom felt his heart lift once more, and he felt like singing along.

And he did. His tongue followed the notes, and next to him he heard Mr. Hu and their other friends joining in. He sang the words as if he had known them his whole life. Once he thought he heard the lovely melody that the phoenix had sung yesterday.

Somewhere in his heart, Tom understood that her song was as old as creation, and perhaps had even been part of the very spell that had created the universe. And it was a song that continued to resonate deep within the world and everything that was a part of it.

He was no longer afraid when the song crept back into a cruel ugliness, because that, too, was part of the world, and he realized now that the loveliness would always return.

He could not have said how long they sang, but he

began to feel a warmth fluttering in his chest like a bird trying to escape a cage. When the Empress tapped him, his body vibrated like a jade chime and sounded a high, musical note that kept on resounding.

From deep within his body slipped a blue light as thin as a piece of yarn. The Empress pulled her hand back and the boy felt something tugging at him. Again the Empress repeated the gesture, drawing the light toward her. Tom felt like a scarf that was being unraveled, yet he felt no pain. He was simply being "unmade."

When the Empress touched each of the other four, they sounded a different note as if they, too, were jade chimes. Nimbly she drew a red ribbon of light that spiraled from Mr. Hu's chest to slide around Tom's blue light while a black light leaped from Mistral's. Monkey's was white, while Sidney's was yellow. The slender threads curled around one another, round and round, until they had merged into a multicolored rope that she caressed and shaped, then wrapped carefully around the horns of the inner pair of dragons.

The Empress leaped into her chariot and, with a click of her tongue, sent the dragons springing into the air, though only the outer pair had wings to flap. As she rose upward, she drew the blazing fibers from each of the five behind her, weaving them together to form a rainbow-colored cable that followed her even as she became only a speck in the distance.

Tom watched in awe as she disappeared into the now cavernous gap in the sky. What could she do against that vastness? But then a multicolored stripe appeared within the darkness, spreading outward until it filled the canyon. And suddenly the last of the colored rope broke its connection to their group and wriggled upward like the tail of a snake. Slowly the iridescence began to deepen into a blue that matched the rest of the sky.

And then the Empress was descending in her chariot, long sleeves fluttering like wings, until the wild dragon team lit upon the ground light as leaves. "Once again you've saved the world, children." She smiled down at them.

Sidney patted himself all over. "Hey, I'm still alive."

The Empress's mouth curled up in a half smile. "I only needed a bit of each of your souls. You have more than enough. Did you think I would take it all?"

"You could have told us," Sidney said as he wiped his forehead with a paw.

"But then I would have missed the expression on your faces." The Empress laughed softly. "After all, I must have my little joke as payment."

"Thank you," was all Tom could say.

Lord and lady, warrior and monster, knelt and touched their heads against the ground.

The Empress basked in their gratitude for a moment and then leaned over the side of her chariot to kiss Tom on the cheek where the scale had been. "Remember, boy, that a treasure becomes even more precious when it is lost."

She shook the misty reins, and her dragon team swept the chariot in a circle, racing faster and faster over the ground, throwing up plumes of blue dust, and finally bounding into the air. Empress, dragons, and chariot disappeared into the chasm.

Rocks thudded and the ground groaned as the earth sealed itself into a ragged, puckered scar to mark where the Empress had healed it, and then the spring fountained up to fill the pond once again.

CHAPTER EIGHTEEN

True to their vow, the Alliance scoured the world for any remnants of Vatten's army. With the defeat of their master, most had the good sense to surrender and were handed over to Lady Torka and the other rebels.

And even though the greatest threat was removed with Vatten's death, everyone, including Master Yen and the Dragon King, conceded that the ancients were wise to leave the phoenix in the care of a Guardian who would resist the temptation of using his powers. And, upon their return to the store, a guard was drawn from the different groups of the Alliance to keep an eye on the store as well as on one another.

When Mr. Hu tried to return the guardianship to her, Mistress Lee refused, stating that she was now retired.

The phoenix hardly budged from his box bed and yet they could find nothing wrong with him physically. All they could do was make him as comfortable as possible. Mistress Lee spent hours with her "great-grandson," reading and singing to him softly.

Despite his worries for the phoenix, Tom threw himself into his studies. Mr. Hu, it turned out, had several college degrees and had begun to homeschool him in regular subjects as well the Lore; and the Guardian proved as exacting a taskmaster in mathematics and grammar as he was on thaumaturgy. Despite her objections, Räv was included in the normal classes as well.

However, she was the one who insisted on taking part in the magic classes. Since she grumbled so much about her regular courses, Tom asked why she was taking on more.

She shrugged defensively. "Well, he's my kid too, you know." And that was how she became Mr. Hu's second apprentice without ever asking or being asked.

For the next six months, their days were divided among lessons, chores, and an ailing phoenix.

By the time the Alliance decided it was safe to celebrate a final victory, the phoenix was no longer a cute ball of fluff—he had grown a full foot in height, most of it in his legs. His feathers could not keep up with his growing body and covered him sparsely. His head appeared too big for his body and a tuft of feathers rose from it like a scarlet cowlick.

Having outgrown his pouch, the gangly bird now rode

on Tom's shoulder as they walked through the flashy, per-fumed gate to Master Yen's restored palace. The promise of a party seemed to renew the phoenix's spirits. So every-one was feeling quite festive—even Mr. Hu, who had received written promises from the Alliance for safe pas-sage back from Master Yen's to his home in Chinatown.

Mr. Hu had loaned the children and Mistress Lee more antique robes, and Räv had insisted on helping him make the choices. She was quite pleased with her red robe with flowers embroidered with gold thread. She had selected a blue one for Tom and a lavender one with a phoenix embroidered on it for Mistress Lee.

Everyone marveled at the remodeled palace that floated high over the Chinese wilderness. Master Yen had taken the opportunity to make it grander, more elaborate, and, of course, gaudier.

Yet, as huge as the central chamber was, it was packed with celebrants glittering with gold and gems. Sidney did a brisk business with the scaled folk who sought his pol-ish openly, despite glares from Mr. Hu.

Master Yen had managed to manufacture even more suan-yü than before, and the trays were piled even higher with food and drink. The apologetic wizard served the phoenix himself—at one point bringing them sweet, bright blue drinks called the Unicorn's Delight. "Do you like them?" Master Yen asked. "I found the enchantment in a rather old codex, written in the margin of some newt recipes."

Mistress Lee brightened. "Oh, I'd love to see them!"

"I'll send you a copy," promised Master Yen.

"Yen, come and dance," Lady Torka shouted with a polite flutter of her wings to greet the phoenix and his companions. The tips of her feathers were gilded for the celebration.

She had to shout because Ch'ih Yu and Lord Trumma had renewed their competition; this time beating drums instead of each other's heads. Lord Harnal was doing his best to get them to stop before they gave everyone headaches—going so far as to prod them with his quills, but they kept on, thumping away enthusiastically as they skipped away from him around and around the drums.

"I'll be right there," Master Yen yelled to Lady Torka, and spreading sleeves as wide as her wings, he flapped over to join her.

K'ua Fu was dancing to the beat of their drums; or rather he stood still while his snakes writhed. Many others, like Monkey, studiously turned away from the unsettling sight.

Despite the noise, they could hear another sound like a truck idling its engine.

"What's that, Mama?" the phoenix asked and imitated the sound.

"That's Grandpa." Tom smiled.

The phoenix listened to the tiger's chest for a moment and then laid his head against the boy's. "No, it's you."

"It's the tiger in you that's purring." Mistress Lee laughed. "It wouldn't let you give up and that's what won the victory."

"Excuse me, Mistress Lee," Mr. Hu corrected her with a shake of his head, "but it wasn't my blood: It was your wisdom."

In a higher level of the room, a dazzled Mistress Quick, her wing quite recovered, sat beside the Dark Lady while the pi fang, falcon, and some of the other heroic birds took turns looping through the air. If Mistress Quick could have blushed with pleasure, Tom was sure she would have.

Räv slid Tom's glass away and crooked her finger for him to lean over so they could talk. "There's one thing that's been bothering me all this time. So 'fess up. What would you have done if our attack hadn't worked? Would you have used Junior as the last resort?"

As Tom squirmed on his stool, Mistress Lee came to his rescue. "It's the heart of the Guardianship."

Räv rolled her eyes. "Oh, please. If I hear that one more time, I'll scream." She jerked her head at Tom. "I mean, with the world at stake, you wouldn't really have sat on your hands, would you? You would have changed your mind and used the phoenix, right?"

Mr. Hu tinked a claw against his own glass. "My

apprentice would have done the right thing," he said firmly.

Tom grinned sheepishly. "If I remember right, Räv was going to pound me for doing that."

Räv folded her arms as she studied him. "Thanks for reminding me." Pulling back her wide sleeve, she raised her fist and swung—but pulled her punch in the last moment so that she merely tapped him on the cheek where the scale had been. "There. Consider it done."

"Okay," Tom said, rubbing the spot—not for the first time since they had returned from China. It was strange to be free of the Empress's blessing—or curse. Sometimes he felt as if a great burden had been lifted and other times he felt unprotected.

"Now, now, none of that," Master Thick said as he paddled down toward them through the air. He moved awkwardly because he was keeping one paw behind his back. When he was floating at their eye level, he cleared his throat. "My wife tells me you broke your club," he said. "That's very careless, my girl."

"But we lost them in a good cause." Räv grinned.

"True enough." The forgiving rat brought out a new club now. "So I've made new ones for the pair of you." He floated shyly as Tom and Räv each examined theirs. "I had time to decorate these while my wife was recovering." He pointed a claw at the carved design on one of them. "That's the Imperfect Mountain."

251

The phoenix rapped the club with his beak with a rare show of excitement. "There you are, Papa. And there you are, Mama."

Tom smiled when he noticed that Mistress Quick looked even bigger and fiercer than Vatten.

Mr. Hu nodded his head politely. "The scene's just like it was."

The gray rat scratched behind his ear. "Is it? I had to imagine what it was like. I should have been there to help."

"We would have finished Vatten even faster," Mr. Hu said kindly.

Master Thick puffed out his chest. "Well, I'm glad to see the Missus get her due." He was clearly enjoying basking in her reflected glory. "And everyone's done handsome by the both of us. But we will be glad to get home. We'll have some cleanup to do for sure."

"You'd be welcome to stay here or anywhere you want," Mr. Hu said.

"It's nice to hobnob with the high and mighty, but home's home," Master Thick declared firmly and waved a paw around. "Not that Mistress Quick couldn't brighten this place up a bit."

"It does lack her touch," the tiger said diplomatically.

"If you're ever in our neighborhood, feel free to visit," Master Thick offered. "Autumn's the best time. The air's cool, but not too cool, and the nuts are all in."

"We'll remember that," Mr. Hu promised.

"Your Highness," the gray rat said, bowing to the phoenix.

"Master Thick," the little bird said, dipping his own head.

As the gray rat started to return to his wife, Sidney chimed in, "Hey, cousin, have you thought about my proposal?"

Master Thick scratched his head. "I don't know if we can make as much as you want."

Sidney sidled in, cozying up to the other rat. "That's because you think small. What you need is an assembly line . . ."

"I don't know that we want a factory in our mountains," Master Thick said uncomfortably.

Monkey snagged Sidney by his tail and snatched him away. "Leave him alone. He's happy as he is."

"Home's home," Master Thick repeated with a grateful nod and swam away.

The phoenix staggered as if he had been hit. "Please don't grab Uncle," he pleaded with Monkey.

"I'm not hurting him," Monkey said.

Sidney looked unconcerned as he glided upside down. "Listen, kiddo. We got to make hay while the sun shines."

The Guardian growled, "That isn't a license to pester the other guests. Can't you forget business for once and enjoy yourself?"

"Business *is* pleasure," Sidney said, trying to tug free from Monkey's grip.

"And I'm telling you to take a vacation no matter how miserable it makes you." Monkey swung the rat gently by his tail as easily as if he were a balloon on a string, bringing him to a halt over the table.

The rat pouted, but then gave in to the inevitable. "Well," he said, picking up a piece of cake from a plate, "I guess I ought to bring the orders up to date and check my inventory."

"Besides," Mr. Hu said as Monkey released the rat, "you should be considering your future plans instead. My paws are going to be rather full training my apprentices, so I've been thinking of taking on a partner to handle the store."

The cake halted just before the rat's mouth. "No kidding."

"You know Hu can't tell a joke to save his life." Monkey chuckled.

Sidney rubbed his muzzle. "Hmm, maybe it's time to move on to the higher-end merchandise. You know, class up my act."

"But no cheating," Mr. Hu warned. "No selling counterfeit Ming vases as the real thing."

Sidney was the picture of innocence. "Oh, I wouldn't think of it, partner."

The Guardian couldn't see that the rat had crossed his paws behind his back, but the others could.

"That's right," the ape whispered to the children. "Sidney doesn't have to think about cheating people. He does it out of instinct."

His cheeks bulging with cakes, the rat sputtered, "You know, Mr. H., if you want to scold someone about being too serious, talk to Mistral. She keeps going around asking everyone if they've seen the Dragon King. She looks so mad that half the people are too scared to answer her. She's waiting by the front door."

"She's still nursing her grudge against him," Monkey said, looking troubled.

"I'd have to be crazy to come between feuding dragons," Mr. Hu said, but he quickly launched himself into the air.

"I think Hu might need our help too," Mistress Lee said as she followed with a kick, and the others swam after her.

"Where's Papa?" the phoenix asked, twisting his head around.

"Go on ahead," Räv panted. The red-faced girl was floundering through the air, doing a good impression of someone drowning.

The phoenix startled Tom by spreading his wings and fluttering away from his shoulder. "You'll get hurt," Tom said, stretching out his hand to grab him.

The phoenix hovered just out of his reach. "I'm fine, Mama," the bird said impatiently.

Tom realized that a chamber where no one could fall was the kindest place for a fledgling to learn how to fly. "Okay, but be careful."

The phoenix began to tug at Räv's sleeve with his beak, but the bird was going to need more help.

"Come on, Papa." Tom grinned and, swimming up on the other side, hooked a hand underneath the girl's arm.

"I can manage by myself," Räv said, twisting free.

"But you don't have to," the phoenix said.

"That's the point of being family," Tom pointed out.

The girl tipped her head, the motion making her tilt backward. "I guess, if it will shut the two of you up."

"Maybe me." Tom smiled. "But I can't speak for Junior."

"Papa moves faster as a blimp," the phoenix teased as he seized her sleeve again, and he and Tom began to tow Räv through the chamber.

Mistress Lee, Mr. Hu, and Sidney set down easily as they entered the corridor, and Monkey landed just as comfortably. The children made a less graceful entrance, plopping down on their stomachs as gravity asserted itself.

The phoenix, however, managed to hover in the air.

"You're flying." Mistress Lee smiled in delight.

"I am?" the phoenix asked and looked down. "I guess I am."

"Now, where's that camera when I need it?" Sidney said, hunting through his fur.

"There isn't time for this." The tiger helped the children to their feet. "We have a friend to save."

Tired by his first attempt at flight, the phoenix settled back upon Tom's shoulder as they trotted down the long, spiraling hallway; but every now and then he experimented with a flap of his wings, reveling in the discovery of a new power.

The dragon had perched herself above the palace's main entrance, staring down like a huge, scaly spider. "Go away," she glowered.

Monkey strode up until he was below her. "We just finished one war," he was pleading. "Don't start another."

Mistral stretched her long neck and squinted menacingly at the ape. "That worm has taken everything from me. Don't tell me you're siding with him now."

Monkey raised both paws hastily. "Not me. But why do you have to start your brawl here, with so many witnesses?"

"You always prided yourself on striking at the right time," Mr. Hu argued, and pointed impatiently at the floor. "So come down from there."

Mistral sighed with exasperation. "How am I expected to ambush someone with all of you standing around like it's a convention?"

"Friends keep other friends from doing foolish things," Mistress Lee scolded.

"Auntie, you can't fight." Rising from Tom's shoulder,

the phoenix wobbled into the air.

For a moment, the dragon forgot her grudge. "Well, look at you! You're growing all the time. It won't be long before we're playing tag in the clouds."

Monkey cleared his throat. "You have to be alive to do that."

"Make way!" proclaimed a loud voice. "Make Way for His Majesty, the Suzerain of the Seven Seas!"

An ornamented Tench was flying toward them, with a half-dozen gold-trimmed dragon warriors as an escort, followed by the largest dragon of all—for the occasion, the Dragon King had put on even more jewels and gold than the last celebration, so that it was a wonder he could move at all. As it was, he flew very slowly.

"Go away!" Mistral whispered to them fiercely.

"The war's over," the phoenix said. "You mustn't hurt anyone anymore. Right, Mama?"

"Uh, right," Tom said. "But remember, if fighting does break out, you can't use your power to stop it."

"Make way!" Tench ordered with an officious sweep of his paw.

But the Dragon King had seen them. "Be more respectful of the Guardian, you fool."

Tench bowed his head abjectly. "A thousand pardons."

Mr. Hu deliberately stepped underneath Mistral so she could not pounce. "And if I had the time, I'd demand you say each one of them."

"Ha, ha, ha," boomed the Dragon King as he swept in over the heads of his escort. "It would serve the toad right, but I didn't think you were *that* bored, Guardian." He nodded his head to the children and Sidney. "But then, what could match the excitement of saving the world?" His head dipped ever so slightly to Monkey as if the recent events had perhaps created a truce between them. "Though how could things be dull with my battle companion?"

"You'd be surprised," Monkey said, keeping his eyes upon Mistral.

With her original ambush spoiled, Mistral crept under the arch and peered out. "We've got unfinished business."

The Dragon King held up a paw as his escort surged forward protectively. "Yes, we do." He appeared strangely calm for someone facing such a deadly foe.

Before Tom could stop him, the phoenix flapped his wings and flew awkwardly between the dragons. "No more fighting."

Mistress Lee strode forward to join him. "Yes, it's time for both of you to act your age."

"Get out of the way," Mistral snarled at her friends.

Mistress Lee folded her arms. "No," she said.

Mistral raised a paw threateningly. "I'll knock you out of the way if I have to."

Suddenly the phoenix shuddered as though he were in intense pain.

As both children rushed to the phoenix, Mistress Lee

gently gathered the weak bird in her hands.

"What's wrong with His Highness?" the Dragon King asked in alarm.

"We're not sure," Tom said, taking the bird from his grandmother and cradling him against his chest. He didn't see Mistress Lee exchange concerned looks with Mr. Hu.

Mistral glanced worriedly at them, and then turned to the Dragon King. "You can't hide anymore, you slimy lizard."

The Dragon King studied his gold-tipped claws. "Before you fling insults at me and add to your crimes, may I introduce you to the newest member of my court?"

Mistral descended from the arch down to the threshold. "Why would I want to meet one of your popinjays?"

"Do you hear that, Your Grace?" the Dragon King called merrily over his shoulder. "She doesn't want to see you."

"Well, there's no use arguing with her then. She's too stubborn to change her mind." The dragon that had been hidden behind the escort now emerged. His scales were edged in gold, and rubies were wound around his neck in a band.

"Ring Neck!" gasped Mistral.

The Dragon King waved a paw. "That's no way to refer to His Grace, the Duke of the Flaming Hills."

"We thought you were dead," Tom said as the phoenix stirred in his arms.

"He was wounded badly in the . . . um . . . misunderstanding," the Dragon King said. "The Healer only recently declared him healthy enough to travel."

Mistral glared at him. "Why didn't you tell me?"

The Dragon King shrugged. "We were hardly on the best of terms."

Ring Neck flew past the King to Mistral. "His Majesty has kindly restored my lands. Will you help me rebuild?"

"The entire kingdom needs you if we are to restore our former glory," the Dragon King said, holding out a paw.

Mistral stared at him. "What makes you think I'd trust you again?"

He gave her a crooked smile. "Because I don't think I'll survive your wrath a third time."

"You could bet your kingdom on that," observed Monkey.

"I wouldn't take that wager," the Dragon King admitted. "Besides, you saved my life, Mistral. That is a debt I cannot forget. Titles and a duchy await you as well."

"I don't care about titles or holdings," Mistral snapped.

"Neither do I," Ring Neck said. "Whether it's in the Dragon Kingdom beneath the sea, or wandering on the land, I'll follow you."

"Your lands and titles will always be waiting for you," the Dragon King promised.

"If you aren't the most annoying dragon. I had my

revenge worked out all nice and neat, and then you had to pop up to ruin everything," Mistral grumbled at Ring Neck, closing her eyes.

The phoenix flapped a wing weakly toward Ring Neck. "Who's he, Mama?"

Cradling the bird in his arms, Tom explained that Ring Neck and Mistral were childhood friends, reunited at last after years of separation and betrayal caused by the Dragon King's mistreatment.

The phoenix listened thoughtfully, and seemed to recover his strength; when Mistral continued to keep her eyes shut, the bird flew over to her with strong beats of his wings. "Are you asleep, Auntie?"

"No, I'm thinking," Mistral sulked, still reluctant to give up her vengeance. "They're asking me to forget a lifetime of grudges."

Mr. Hu clapped his paws together. "In the meantime, there's a party going to waste."

"Yes, why don't you have some refreshments while you decide whether to rip out his throat?" Monkey said.

The Dragon King shook one of his legs. "If you do that, you'll deprive the world of such a fine dancer."

Mistral's eyes snapped open. "Bah! As I recall, you have four left paws."

"His Majesty has taken lessons from me," Ring Neck said.

Mistral reared her head. "I have to see the results

myself. I challenge you to a dance-off. And may the best dancer win."

"Gladly, Your Grace," the Dragon King said, with a touch of relief.

Mr. Hu loosened his tie. "And then I'll dance with you," he roared in delight.

And the Guardian did indeed. A jig, in fact.

CHAPTER NINETEEN

The battle at the Imperfect Mountain was nothing compared to their exertions at the party; and it took several days for everyone to recuperate. Tom and Räv were kept busy rubbing Sidney's miracle ointment on everyone's aching joints.

Upon their return to Chinatown, the phoenix began to sicken again, growing steadily worse with each day, and there was nothing Mr. Hu or Mistress Lee could do for him. The ailing bird spent day and night watching television.

The children read everything they could in Mr. Hu's library, from Ko Hung's *Guide to Magical Beings* to *Metaphysical Nutrition*, for some way to help the bird.

Sidney had his own thoughts about a cure. "It's not good for the kid to sit all day watching TV. He ought to work out a little." The yellow rat puffed as he ran in place beside the table where they were reading. He had taken to jogging around the store to lose some of the weight from the celebration; and though he claimed that he had already dropped several pounds, his thick fur made it impossible to tell.

It was also, the children suspected, a not too subtle hint to Mr. Hu that he should invest in an exercise room. The industrious rat had pointedly left catalogs all around the store and apartment. Mr. Hu had just as resolutely ignored them.

"I've tried to turn off the set," Tom said, glancing worriedly at the bird who was lying upon Mistress Lee's lap while he gazed at the television screen.

Räv made a face at the memory. "And did he ever throw a tantrum."

"Maybe we could distract him if we got another bird to play with him," Tom said.

"Well, no pigeons," Sidney said firmly. "They'll teach him how to swear."

Tom was surprised when the phoenix himself tapped the remote that turned off the television. The sudden silence was almost as unnerving as the bird's eyes when he turned toward the boy.

"Is something wrong?" Tom asked.

The bird glanced at Mistress Lee and then fluttered weakly over to the table to land near the book that Tom had been consulting. "Mama, we need to talk."

"Of course," Tom said.

The phoenix slipped his beak beneath the book's cover and shut it. "I need to talk to the whole family."

When Tom saw how serious the phoenix was, he asked Sidney to go into the basement to fetch Monkey, Mistral, and Ring Neck. Then he went up to the attic where Mr. Hu was busy inventorying the contents.

The tiger set down his clipboard. "Mistress Lee and I have been expecting something like this since the party, but it was up to the phoenix to tell us in his own words." Mr. Hu padded softly down the steps as Tom followed him.

There wasn't much room in the apartment with the two dragons there, so Monkey had to perch upon a cabinet while Sidney squatted on the table with the phoenix. When the apprentice and the Guardian had taken their seats next to Räv and Mistress Lee, the phoenix lifted his head with great dignity, but the words would not come. Only tears.

Mr. Hu took the handkerchief from his breast pocket and held it out to the bird. With twists of his head, the phoenix brushed his eyes against the handkerchief, wiping away his tears. "I wanted a family so badly," the bird said.

"And now you have one," Sidney assured him.

"I hate to lose you," the phoenix said, lifting his head.

"We're not going anywhere," Tom said.

"But I have to," the bird whispered.

"But you're safe now," Räv said.

The little bird shook his head and the tuft of feathers waved back and forth. "Vatten may be gone, but I've watched the television with Great-grandmom. Humans are still killing one another the way they always have. I was born too soon. The world isn't ready for me yet."

"Give them time," Tom said.

The phoenix gazed up at his mother. "Do you want me to make the world peaceful, Mama?"

Tom swallowed. "No, of course not."

The phoenix drew its claws slowly back and forth across the tabletop. "Peace isn't in everyone's hearts—not even in my family's. When Auntie wanted to fight at the palace, I felt such pain."

Mistral shifted on her haunches, embarrassed. "But I settled my differences with the king."

The phoenix nodded to the television. "I feel hate and anger everywhere, and my body hurts more and more."

"And it will only get worse as you grow." Mistress Lee sighed. "As you mature, you will become more sensitive until . . ."

"Until I can't stand it," the phoenix finished.

"So what do you want to do?" Tom asked, his voice shaking.

"I . . . I think I should go to sleep again," the phoenix said.

Tom had thought his world had ended when he

believed his grandmother had died; and now it felt like it was ending again. He didn't want the bird to suffer, but he couldn't lose him either. "No, I won't let you."

"Please don't look at me like that, Mama," the bird said.

Tom appealed to Mr. Hu. "Tell him he can't."

The Guardian held the handkerchief so the phoenix could wipe his eyes again. "The conclusion is inescapable, but it was a decision you had to reach yourself. I was wondering how long it would take you." Despite his logical words, there was an ache in his voice.

"Don't you love us?" Räv asked the bird.

The phoenix fluttered to the girl's shoulder and nuzzled a feathery cheek against hers. "It's *because* I love you."

Mistress Lee drew in a deep breath. "Use your heads and not your hearts," she told the children.

"Grandpa and Great-grandma are right," the phoenix said. "You know they are."

Tom had the strange feeling that they had switched roles, and the phoenix was acting like the parent now.

Räv turned with a sob to Tom. "Tell him you won't allow it."

Tom felt helpless. And yet he had never been more sure about what was right. "I can't."

The phoenix rose into the air. "Thank you, Mama. I knew you'd understand."

Räv had started to cry openly. "Oh, Tom. Why can't you do what's wrong for a change?"

Mr. Hu was choked up himself. "Because he's the stuff from which Guardians are made."

"Yes, he is," the phoenix said, settling on the tiger's shoulder.

Tom used his sleeve to dab at his eyes while the phoenix flew around the room saying his good-byes to the others. He realized the Empress had tried to warn him when she said a treasure became more precious when you lost it.

The phoenix landed on Tom's shoulder. "You won't be alone. I'll always be with you."

"I'll be here too," Räv promised. "Waiting for you."

"And if not us," Tom swore, "then we'll find someone who will care for you just as much as we do."

The phoenix's wings caressed him like a soft breeze. "I know."

Tom looked over at his grandmother and Mr. Hu. "What do we need for the transformation spell?"

Mistress Lee spread her hands. "My great-grandchild will know everything instinctively."

With a flap of his wings, the phoenix landed upon the table, his claws clicking across the top until he took his place in the center. Lifting his head, he opened his beak and began to trill, his voice rising higher and higher as if he were soaring up to the stars themselves, and each note felt like a feather tickling Tom's ears.

It was a song far different than the Empress's and yet the boy knew it was as old. The song wrapped itself around his heart, warm and comforting as a blanket on a cold night. And any doubts and fears he felt evaporated inside that warmth.

As the bird sang, it began to pirouette, with wings spread and tail feathers fanned out. The turns were slow and stately, like the procession of the planets and stars in the sky, as sure as the sun will replace the moon each dawn—and that someday, peace will follow war everywhere in the world.

The bird began to whirl faster and faster until suddenly the tune grew faint and an egg appeared upon the table, the notes coming faintly through the shell until the tune ended at last.

Tom felt an ache in his chest and he let his breath out slowly.

"Geez, wasn't that something?" Sidney rubbed his eyes.

Mr. Hu set his paws on either side of the egg. "It's customary for the Guardian to choose the disguise for the phoenix. But I am open to suggestions, Master Thomas."

Tom thought back to that day when the phoenix had wandered loose in Chinatown. It seemed like ages ago. "He"—the boy's voice failed him and it took him a moment to find it again—"he liked stars."

"Yes, like crystals in the night sky," Räv agreed.

"Then a star it shall be," Mr. Hu said. "Do you hear us, Your Highness?"

There was a soft red glow within the egg and suddenly they were looking at a crystal star. His hand trembling, Tom picked it up. He would watch over his child all his days; and he also remembered what the Empress had said about souls being reborn.

"We'll meet again one day," Tom said. "If not in this life, then in another."

Within the crystal, he thought he saw a fiery smile flash in answer.

AFTERWORD

I was living in Buffalo when I began writing my first Chinese American novel in the Golden Mountain Chronicles, *Dragonwings*. I was terribly homesick there and I wanted to return at least in my imagination, if not in body, to the place that I considered home, San Francisco's Chinatown.

At the same time I worked on *Dragonwings*, I was working on my dissertation on William Faulkner. I think one of the things that attracted me to his work was the way he had transformed his real home into an imaginary one, Yoknapatawpha County.

Something similar happened to me: The Chinatown that I had known as a child was an intimate one, where everyone knew one another, and it was the same way with the one in my head. The characters all knew one another and introduced me to them.

However, my boyhood Chinatown was not quite the same as my grandmother's Chinatown. She wanted me to think of her as a modern American woman, but her superstitions provided glimpses into a different, more magical world.

So, just as the Chinatown of the Golden Mountain Chronicles reflects the real one, I've tried to make the Chinatown of Tom and Mr. Hu reflect my grandmother's magical home—where ghosts, imps, and monsters hid in the shadows.